DREAM
WATCHER

ALEXIS CASTELLE

DREAM
WATCHER

TATE PUBLISHING
AND ENTERPRISES, LLC

Published by Tate Publishing & Enterprises, LLC
127 E. Trade Center Terrace | Mustang, Oklahoma 73064 USA
1.888.361.9473 | www.tatepublishing.com

Tate Publishing is committed to excellence in the publishing industry. The company reflects the philosophy established by the founders, based on Psalm 68:11,
"The Lord gave the word and great was the company of those who published it."

Book design copyright © 2016 by Tate Publishing, LLC. All rights reserved.
Cover design by Norlan Balazo
Interior design by Richell Balansag

Published in the United States of America

ISBN: 978-1-68301-171-2
Fiction / African American / Christian
16.04.15

To the Henry/Howard family: Thanks for allowing me to be part of the *best* family for all these years. Love you all on purpose, now and always.

Special thank you to my Hobbs crew, Suzanne, Ron, Jay, Cathie, Jamie, Jimmy, Davina, Daniel, Matt, Teirrah, Sylvia, Melissa, Tim W., Tim Sr., Tim Jr, and Jason: Thank you for your support and for demonstrating such awesome love. My heart holds you all close even when my arms cannot.

I love all of you for filling my life with many special seasons.

And the king said unto them, I have dreamed a dream, and my spirit was troubled to know the dream.

—Daniel 2:3

Contents

GROWING PAINS

Freaknik was the trumpet-blowing party announcing spring break in Atlanta. It was the end of four laborious years. She was finally ready to really let her hair down and have a little fun. Over the years, upon hearing about the antics at the Spelman-Morris Brown picnics, she felt that might be letting loose more than she was ready to. Yet, Chimere was determined to let loose a little before she graduated.

Attending parties had been almost nonexistent between her studies, her tutoring, and her Alpha Kappa Alpha duties. The invitations came, but she always had a test to study for or a paper to write. Those were the reasons she'd depend upon. At the unrelenting urging of Kelly, her best friend and soror, Chimere finally agreed to go spring break of 1985, but only to one of the after parties. The black fraternities' reputation for hosting some of the best Freaknik after-parties was growing. The best known and most talked about were the parties at the Omega Psi Phi house.

Chimere and Kelly spent an entire morning at the beauty shop getting press and curls. Leaving the early afternoon to browse downtown, looking for the perfect top to wear with the required black shorts. Chimere found a backless sequined baby-pink top and pink jeweled earrings that hung to her shoulders. Kelly found a cute low V-cut apple-green halter and matching bangle-sized hoop earrings. Since they wore the same size shoe, it wasn't necessary to shoe shop, which for them was usually an all-day escapade. Since their meeting in second grade, they had been practically inseparable.

Chimere was more inquisitive, slightly introverted, and very studious. She found her voice easily on issues pertaining to middle class objectives and the impoverished. She had a way of swaying almost every conversation into a discussion of politics. Kelly often teased her saying that she would become president one day. Her ability to give statistics about the lack of affordable housing, unemployment, or any economic issues would leave most audiences speechless. Always at the ready to share numerous ideas on how to make the social services systems more a service than a hindrance. Chimere was five foot four with golden-brown skin tone, and thick wavy light-brown hair she always kept neatly in a bun at the base of her neck. Her rounded ebony eyes were framed by thick black lashes, and dimples visible with the slightest curve of her full lips.

Kelly was outgoing, boisterous, and always the life of the party. Although she was only five feet tall, she always had the personality, confidence, and strut of a runway model. Her smooth chocolate-brown complexion blended well with the jet black ringlets curled just below her shoulders. It was her emerald-green speckled eyes that turned heads initially, but her voice made it difficult not to stare. She had a powerful and soulful voice, and she knew every song by Minnie Riperton, Donna Summer, and Anita Baker. Once she began to sing, all eyes were on her in amazement.

With new shirts, new hairdos, and light makeup, they were ready for whatever the night held for them. Chimere was not a drinker, however, she needed very little encouragement tonight. Kelly burst into laughter when Chimere took the flask and chugged it.

"Whoa! Slow down girlfriend! "Kelly said giggling." You know that's not soda pop, right?"

With her face twisted, mouth open, and breathing heavily, Chimere said, "Yeah, I know. You told me. What the heck is it? Phew, It's burning my heart out!" They laughed. Chimere took another swig and shook her head. "Ugh! Is my hair down yet?"

The street was full of mingling people and honking car horns when they reached the house. After locating a spot for parking a few houses down, Kelly was glad she had her VW Beetle. They could hear "Single Life" by Cameo welcoming them to the party. They danced their way to a homemade tropical-style bar. Jim "Jumbo" Smalls, an Omega Psi Phi frat brother and Kelly's boyfriend of three years, greeted them.

Jumbo was just the opposite of his nickname. He stood six foot two and thin as a toothpick. His upper arms and calves were very muscular from eight or more years of playing basketball. His short curly black hair looked like little knots showing his almost-white scalp. He was a pale shade of yellow with squinty brown eyes and thick curled lashes. A neatly trimmed mustache topped his full pink lips. When he smiled, his eyes would just about disappear. His voice was a deep baritone, and his laugh was contagious.

He handed each girl a tall plastic cup filled with a greenish-yellow beverage. He kissed Kelly then took both girls by the hand and led them through the backyard. There were clusters of people spread throughout, and the music was earsplitting. The yard was decorated with purple-and-gold streamers. Gold tablecloths covered the tables that were lining the right side of the yard. Along the back fence, three hot tubs had been brought in. All were already filled and surrounded by bathing suit-clad girls of all shades, shapes, and sizes. Some girls were hanging out dancing by the booth setup, where DJ Killer was spinning the week's top ten mix.

Jumbo looped arms with each of the girls and proudly strutted through the yard. Just as they were greeting fellow frats and sorors, Prince's "Let's Go Crazy" boomed, sending the yard into a frenzy. The girls were pulled toward the center of the yard and on to a dance floor made up of painted purple sheets of plywood.

The evening was filled with laughter, dancing, and liquor. Every once in a while, the skunky aroma of marijuana would fill the air. As the sky grew darker and tiki torches were lit, couples began to form. DJ Killer began playing ballads by Freddy Jackson, Teddy Pendergrass, and Luther Vandross, setting a mood for romance.

After dancing to several songs, winded and a little light-headed Chimere found her way to an empty table. Kelly was barefoot on the dance floor with Jumbo. Chimere was resting her head in her hands when she felt a tender yet firm grip on her shoulders. She turned to find Theron standing over her with a big smile on his face. She smiled up at him. He pulled her to her feet and led her to the dance floor. Chimere enjoyed the platonic relationship she had with Theron. She liked having him around, mostly because he made it easy for her to stave off all the unwanted advances. She also enjoyed how most of their conversations had an air of debate to them. They met the beginning of her sophomore year during rush week at an Omega-sponsored step show. Theron resembled a young Muhammad Ali. She was pledging Alpha Kappa Alpha, and he was pledging Alpha Phi Alpha. He was a sophomore studying science and medicine at Morehouse.

Their meeting turned into a debate over the lack of adequate medical resources available to underemployed Americans and how misguided and undertrained the employees of these agencies; the people who held the direction of social services in their hands. His prospective was simple in regards to racism. He was having difficulty with the concept of any person, race, or ethnicity being superior. He believed the superior group was only superior because they had the power to withhold and/or dominate. It angered him how the Caucasian media seem to spotlight the most degrading and stereotypical African Americans as often as possible. He believed that African Americans—although still being exploited—were a re-evolving group of people. Despite being ripped away from their comfort zone to a life filled with barricades, withholding of opportunities, very limited rights, being treated worse than animals, and only educated in areas of servitude. Now finally able to freely demonstrate their numerous talents and abilities, both as individuals and as a group. Like any other group given the right tools to dominate and excel in all areas, they were rebuilding and developing their traditions with and without religion. He compared the life of most African Americans to the life of prisoners of war or an abused person. He felt some of the negative behaviors demonstrated by less educated African Americans were a direct result of being deprived access to jobs with reasonable pay, quality education, and quality housing.

He would often say, "What do you expect when you keep a dog caged and hungry? Of course when he gets out, he goes a little berserk and will do some serious damage. It is deprivation that is evil, not the color of the person's skin."

Theron was handsome, smart, funny, and always willing to lend a hand. Though Chimere had made it clear she was not interested in any type of serious relationship, he kept coming around. She explained that getting in a serious relationship was not part of her short-term goals. He conceded, but he made sure to keep himself in her line of vision. He made it a point of being at her apartment and waiting on her at least twice a week to take her out to eat or to any of the Greek events. He knew she would always try to say she was too busy. Most of the time though, despite his best reasoning, she would decline. He did his best to be nonchalant on those rare times she would agree.

As a welcome-back present in their junior year, he gave her a new word-processing Brother typewriter. He had made it clear his plan was to stick around as long as she would allow. He was content just being with her. Most of their time together would be at her place studying. He would either be lying on the floor or slouched on the couch in the living room, while she would be seated at the desk or sitting sideways in the oversized armchair. She could catch him often staring in a dreamy trance as she was typing a paper or reading.

Chimere was impressed and grateful for such a thoughtful gift. Now she wouldn't have to spend hours on the typewriter at the library. In her junior year she was more determined to stay focused on reaching her goals. Thankfully, Theron's gift helped to keep her from being distracted from wearing an honors collar and getting her degree.

Theron was certain he would be able to convince her by their senior year. He had to convince her without a doubt, he was the man for her. He was glad the Omegas were hosting the last party before finals, freeing Theron to show Chimere how serious he was. His stocking job at Kroger had provided enough money for him to pay for his books and put aside money to buy a ring from one of the local pawnshops. As he was taking a drink of courage, he fumbled with the jewelry box in his pocket.

The limbo started. Kelly came and swept Chimere away to join in. They each took a spot in one of the two lines, bouncing until it was their turn to dance Soul Train-style down to the bar. Laughingly, Kelly began to shimmy under the two-foot-high bar. Giggling, Chimere followed suit. When she stood, she found herself face to face with a most handsome six-foot-three barricade, Medan "Da'Man" Freeman. Medan, a popular alumni Omega Psi Phi brother, was captivated by Chimere. He hadn't planned on staying, but the glimmer of her shirt and her beautiful dimpled smile made him feel like his feet weighted a ton. He wasn't in any rush to get away now. She was worth missing any appointment he might have had.

"Well, well, well. Finally, some AKAs who can bring it and hang!" Medan didn't move nor take his eyes off Chimere. Chimere didn't budge. She stood her ground with her hands on her hips and lips pursed. "Hey, Jumbo! Who is this newbie? She's quite the little hottie. I'm loving those dimples." He laughed at the smirk on her face and then he mimicked her stance.

Chimere shifted her weight trying to keep her balance, sucked her bottom lip, and rolled her eyes. He placed his finger under her chin and smiled. "Hot dog! Miss lady has attitude too! That's what I'm talking about. Sexy, smart, beautiful, and feisty."

Jumbo looked up from his overflowing plate of barbeque. "Oh, hey, Da'Man! What's going on? Been a while, Bro." Jim took another bite of rib bone, smacking loudly as he cleaned his fingers of the barbeque sauce. "Medan, this is Chi-Chi. She's a senior and a political geek. I know you've probably seen her at the carwashes and stuff. She's my girl KeKe's soror and best friend."

Chimere was at a loss for words as she stared at this gorgeous black Adonis blocking her movement. In her mind, he was well-suited to his nickname. He was Da Man! Composing herself, she stepped to her left to pass.

While Medan didn't take his eyes off her, he moved to his right without effort, keeping them face to face.

"Excuse me, Da'Man, but you're in my way. You're quite a big fella." She patted him on the chest as she swayed. "I would very much appreciate it if you would allow me to pass."

Medan struggled to keep from laughing, but her sincerity and gentleness tickled him. "Well, since you put it like that." He stood his ground and laughed even harder, watching her frustration causing her cheeks to flush red. "I'm sorry, little momma, but you have to know the password to get by."

Chimere looked at him and tilted her head from side to side. "Password? Hmmm. This should be easy. You're a Neanderthal and most likely live in a cave. I would say the password must be the species you belong to—Chogalodite!"

Medan and his boys broke out in thunderous laughter. Everyone around them laughed. Chimere giggled, smiled at him, again patted him on his huge chest. She walked by them all to the table where Kelly was nursing a scrape on her elbow. Kelly was wide-eyed and snickering as her friend came to sit next to her.

"Whoa, Chi-Chi! You got one over on Da'Man! Girl, I know you've heard those stories about him, right? He's Da'Man, the Omega president a couple of years ago, the one with the reputation of being a tough guy and a player. He was truly living up to the nickname of the Omega's, a Que-Dog in every sense. He took it even further after graduation and got hooked up with the BMC in Atlanta. I can't believe he let you just walk away like that. You actually made him laugh. You're going to be a legend on the Spelman campus. Skee-wee!"

Chimere squealed as she tilted her head to the side, "Skee-wee!" They laughed as she helped tend the scrape on Kelly's elbow. "Well, Da'Man should have checked before he messed with Da'Woman!" They laughed again. "What's BMC?"

Jumbo came over to the table with three full cups of the greenish-yellow beverage. The DJ had switched back to dance music. Chaka Khan's "I Feel for You" blasted through the yard. Just as they were about to toast, Da'Man came up behind Jumbo. Jumbo turned to greet him with the Omega handshake and handed him the drink he had for himself.

"So, li'l miss Chi-Chi, you got me on that one." Medan took the seat next to Chimere. He leaned in close as he whispered, "Sorry to interrupt. Mind if I join you?"

Chimere scooted her chair away from Medan. Looking into his handsome face, she smiled. "No, not at all. We were just going to toast you, as a matter of fact. Everyone have a drink? Okay, here's to Da'Man for knowing he can't outsmart Da'Woman!"

They tapped their cups together, laughing. The crowd erupted with Greek calls, and cheers went forth. Medan noticed Chimere had moved her chair so he easily moved his seat closer to Chimere. Theron and several of his brothers came over to the table. Theron steered the discussion to last basketball season and the upcoming football season. The more heated the conversation got, the closer Thereon would move to Chimere, as more of the Alpha brothers huddled around. Kelly and Chimere decided to go over to the DJ booth to make a few song requests and spend time with Killer.

Medan caught Chimere by the arm as they were getting up to leave. "Hold up, baby girl, I'm not done with you." He pulled her into his lap and placed his large hand at the base of her bare back.

Theron tensed, but he knew he had to keep his mouth shut and his temper under control out of respect. The more Medan rubbed Chimere's back and caressed her thigh, the more he felt his face heat up. It was moments like this he hated frat protocol and rules. He wanted to snatch Chimere off his lap and tell Medan she was his girl. Certainly now stepping to Medan he would be inviting greater embarrassment and most likely a beat down with a night in jail.

The rumble of motorcycles out front shook the walls. For some, it was the signal the party was really about to start. Peabo's sultry voice was belting out "If Ever You're in

My Arms Again" throughout the yard. Medan, with very little effort, carried Chimere to the dance floor.

Theron was steaming, wanting to push through the crowd and pull Chimere away. Her reaction to this man angered and surprised him. For the first time, she didn't seem to mind being groped and fondled. The more Medan rubbed her bare back, the more irritated Theron became. His thoughts were moving more in the direction of violent behavior he had not participated in since grade school. The mixture of alcohol, jealousy, and anger were taking him to a place he thought he left behind.

His mind was whirling, and his thoughts were turning dark. After finishing his drink, he decided it would be best to leave before he did something he would regret. Seething all the way home as images of Medan caressing Chimere almost blinded him. The more he replayed her behavior and how sweetly she was treating Medan, the more his blood boiled. In the years he had known her, she never drank alcohol. Tonight, though, she was drinking like a thirsty camel. She was actually ignoring him. She was all wrapped up in the attention she was getting from Medan. He'd come too far, and he was too close to his degree. It wasn't worth losing his standing with Morehouse or his frat to fight over a girl. He figured with a clearer head in the morning, he would be able to speak to Chimere. Giving the alcohol time to wear off was the best solution, so he went straight to bed.

Medan held Chimere tightly as "Suddenly" by Billy Ocean began to play. Looking down at Chimere's flushed face warmed his heart. Each lyric gave him a new sensation as she pressed into to him. He already enjoyed her quick wit and sarcastic quips, it didn't hurt she was naturally beautiful. Her long dark eyelashes didn't need the light coat of mascara, and her natural peach lips made him want to kiss her until he had to come up for air. He didn't want the music to stop. Holding her in his arms felt more like a replacement of his missing rib. All he could think of was how good he felt at that moment, holding this beautiful, feisty woman in his arms. After the music stopped, Medan held her until she slowly untangled herself from his embrace and made her way back to the table.

She sat and watched as he greeted the group of leather-clad men. He talked to them for a few minutes before they headed out of the yard. The roar of the motorcycles echoed and melted into the night as he made his way to her. She watched as he made his way in her direction.

He wanted to take full advantage of this opportunity to be alone with her. When he sat down, she got up and moved to the other side of the table.

"Hey, why are you sitting way over there?"

"Because I like this side of the table, thank you very much." As she kept looking in the direction of the dance floor.

"Oh, so it's like that now? Now you're going to act like you didn't enjoy sitting on my lap? You sure didn't try to move off before I carried you to the dance floor. You'd have to be one great actress for me to believe you weren't enjoying being in my arms on dance floor."

"Oh, I'm not going to act like I didn't like it. Your lap felt better on my bare legs than these hard chairs, so why should I have moved? Plus, it gave me a better view of that fine brother on the other side of the yard." Chimere pointed in a direction and laughed as she ran her fingers through the last of the dwindling curls. "Dancing with you was refreshing. Actually, you only stepped on my foot twice."

She couldn't help smile at the scowl on Medan's face. He was very handsome, but she really didn't want any distractions. He kept his hair short and his goatee nicely trimmed. His skin reminded her of smooth and creamy caramel on an apple. If she allowed herself, she could get caught up in his almond-shaped chocolate brown eyes beneath dark-tapered eyebrows. He was built specifically to play defensive end, which he had since he was six. He told her his mother recognized his superior athletic ability at a young age. It was her who found the teams for him to play football with. He had always been bigger than most of the kids his age. She soon realized Theron and everyone else had left them at the table alone.

"So you dismissed your entourage, I see." Chimere rested her chin on her folded arms. "Were those your BMC buddies? What is BMC anyway? You would have been better off having them stay. They made you more interesting."

"Dang, girl, you're a cold fish! Yes, as a matter of fact, those were my brothers from my motorcycle club—all Omega alumni. Where have you been…in a closet or something? Everybody around here knows BMC is the Black Motorcycle Community. I just want to get to know you without all my boys trying to make a play for you. With my boys around, it would have been awkward for you. Is that so wrong?"

"Well, not everyone! Some of us take our education very seriously. Some of us are here for more than just the parties and not looking to be somebody's groupie. No, it's not wrong. There you go, *assuming* I want to let you get to know me. You don't even know if I'm seeing anyone. A little presumptuous, don't you think?"

"Girl, please, what woman, unless she's—excuse my language—a slut, would sit on another man's lap if she has a man?"

"Well, stranger things have happened to women when they've had a little too much alcohol—especially one who doesn't drink."

"For a nondrinker, you sure handle your liquor pretty well. I would have never guessed you were a teetotaler the way you've been slamming them back."

"Like the saying goes, never judge a book by its cover! It's been entertaining meeting you, Da'Man. Thanks for the dance." She smiled and patted him on the shoulder. "I really need to find my friend and get home."

"But it's not even midnight! You've got to be joking, right? What are you, Cinderella or something? Come on stay a little longer. I promise I won't bite…well, not hard anyway. I'm really a good guy. Just give me a chance."

"Good guy or bad guy, it doesn't matter either way, really. I've got finals next week. I'm really trying to graduate and keep my Summa Cum Laude status, if that's all right with you."

"Now I really am intrigued. You're evidently very smart as well as beautiful. Seriously, Chi-Chi, are you dating and is it possible for me to fit into your schedule? I would really like you to give me a chance in different surroundings. I can see you're a woman with many layers, and I'd like to enjoy peeling all of them." He chuckled as he stands with hand extended to take her hand. "Seriously, I would be honored if you'd let me take you out to dinner or a movie."

"Really, I'm flattered, but I'm not interested. I'm not some new kid to frat life, and your reputation—well, let's just say, I don't think we would have much in common without the liquor. Just so you know, your reputation at Morehouse is pretty tame in comparison to some of the BMC exploits. I've heard about the crazy soirees. I understand you're now this major player in the Atlanta Black Motorcycle Community."

"You really shouldn't believe everything you hear. You know how stories can get a life of their own as they spread. The fair thing to do is to give me a chance and find out for yourself."

"You have a point, but honestly, I don't have time right now. Maybe after finals, after graduation, we can try to get together...but I make no promises. My calendar is pretty full."

"After graduation? So you're staying in Atlanta? Cool! Then do you, at least, think you have time to speak on the phone? May I get your phone number?"

"Yes, I'm staying in Atlanta. As a matter of fact, I have a job lined up after graduation. Yeah, I guess I can do that."

Chimere reached over, pulled the pen out of his shirt pocket, ripped a matchbook cover she found on the table, and wrote her number down. As she turned to leave, he reached for her hand and pulled her to him. He lightly kissed her on the cheek and took the matchbook. She smiled at him and gently placed her hand on his cheek. "You take care, Da'Man."

"Good night, my sweet, until you let me in! We *will* be talking soon."

"I hope you're not as corny next time we do."

They laughed, and Chimere walked away. She found Kelly and Jumbo sitting by the hot tub with plates full of barbeque. Kelly had sauce all around her mouth. Her eye makeup smeared, making her look like a raccoon, and her hair was puffy and frizzy, which caused Chimere to start laughing. She looked from Kelly to Jumbo and then sat next to Kelly. Gently, she coaxed her intoxicated friend to her feet. They kissed Jumbo on each cheek, then arm-in-arm they headed to the street and home for the night. Chimere was glad this party was close to their apartment, and she had begun to sober up. This time of year, the Atlanta Police were always patrolling around the colleges, just waiting to catch someone driving drunk. Chimere helped Kelly into her bed. Just as she was heading to her room the phone rang. She shook her head and laughed as she answered the phone.

"Hello, Theron."

"Wait! How did you know it was me? You just getting home? So I take it, you had a good time after I left?"

"Ron, you can't be serious! Going and having a good time was the whole idea, remember? Who else would dare call me at this time of night? Yes, we are just getting home. Kelly was a little out of it, so it took me a minute to get her together."

"Yeah, I guess so. So what's up with you and Da'Man? He was all over you, and you seemed to like it."

"Really? If you called here trying to act like the jealous boyfriend, I will hang up right this minute. You've been a good friend and we have fun hanging out. Don't act like this, please! Chill out, man, I know this isn't how you want to end the year. Is that why you left the party without saying good-bye? Because I was having fun with someone other than you?"

"Chi, why are you treating me like this? Treating me like I've not been there for you? And it wasn't just someone else, it was another man—a man you just met, and you let him feel you up and crap. You know how I feel about you!" His voice got deeper as he got louder. "You think I've been hanging around three years because I just want to be friends? I love you and know you feel the same, but the way you were acting really makes me question. You know how many girls I've turned down just to be with you?"

"Of course I'm very fond of you, Theron, but I wouldn't say I love you. If I did, it would be a platonic thing. I never made you turn away anyone. That was your choice. I think we both need to get some sleep. Good night, Ron. We'll discuss this tomorrow when you're sober." She hung up, turned the ringer off, and went to take a shower.

The next morning, Chimere was awakened by loud banging on the apartment door. She was angered when she glanced at her clock, seeing it was barely eight o'clock. She knew it had to be Theron. She grabbed her pink silk robe and hurried to the door. She looked through the peep hole and there was Theron, just as she thought. She decided to not open the door.

"Theron, what the heck do you think you're doing? Go home! It's way too early on a Sunday to be dealing with this. Go home! I will call you later."

"Chi-Chi, I'm not leaving until we talk this over. You owe me at least that. So just open the door, and let's talk about this."

"I'm tired and have splitting headache, so now is not a good time. Go home, and I will walk over when I'm feeling a little better."

"OPEN THE DAMN DOOR!"

"Go home, Theron!"

Chimere headed back to her room while he continued yelling and banging on the door. She was just about to lay her head on her pillow when she heard the crash. She sat up and thought, *No, he couldn't! He wouldn't break down the door.* Then she heard him coming down the hallway. She reached for the phone just as he burst in her room.

"I know he's in here with you? Where is he?" He yanked open her closet pushing aside her clothes to look. Then he threw back her covers and looked under the bed. "I know that's why you didn't want to let me in. Where is he?"

"What are you looking under the bed for? You think any man I'd have in my room would be afraid of you?" Still holding the phone, she rose to her knees. "Ron, you need to get the hell out of my room and my house before I call the police. What is the matter with you? Why are you acting like this?"

His face was sweating, and he was yelling in her face. "Why am I acting like what? Chimere, I have loved you and been waiting for you to let me make love to you for over two years. Then you allow some dude to just sweep you up like a ragdoll, and you ask me that stupid question. What, am I not big enough for you?"

Theron yanked the phone from her hand and slammed it on the cradle. Then he snatched Chimere out of the bed and threw her into her open closet. Slowly, he walked over to her and grabbed her again. Her silence and the defiant look in her eyes only angered him more. He slapped her hard across the face. Chimere screamed for him to stop, but the more she fought him, the more brutal he became. He was yelling at her as he pummeled his fist into her upper body and face. Even though she had stopped screaming, he continued to slam fists into her face and body.

Kelly stirred, hearing the screams. At first, she thought she was still drunk or maybe Chimere was watching something on television. Then she realized the voice she heard was Theron, and the screams were coming from Chimere's room. Kelly jumped out of her bed, not stopping to put on clothes, and ran to Chimere's room.

Seeing Theron beating her best friend, she fought her first impulse to jump on his back. Instead, she grabbed the phone and called the police. After she frantically told them the problem, she dropped the phone. Half-naked, frightened, and angry, she grabbed the first heavy object within her reach and slammed him over the head. The force of the large political science book sent him reeling into the mirror that was hanging on the door. Shards of glass went flying. The jagged edge of the mirror caught Theron above his left brow and sliced across his nose to just under his right eye. Blood was gushing and spraying everywhere, but Kelly kept slamming the book on any part of him she could make contact with.

Tears were streaming down her face, but the sight of her friend, bleeding and limp, stopped her momentarily, then his movement made her angrier. She raised the book and started beating Theron more. She whacked him twice in the face. At the second whack, she heard the crack of his nose breaking, but she just couldn't stop swinging. She was about to hit him again when she felt a strong hand pull her back.

"Ma'am, please put down the book."

Kelly looked from the police officer to the bloody book in her hand and dropped to her knees. Chimere was being looked over by the paramedic, but she wasn't moving. Kelly looked at the police officer and saw his mouth moving, but she couldn't hear any words. She looked back at her friend being strapped to the stretcher. After a moment, she found her feet beneath her and ran to her side. The paramedic held out an arm to halt her. The police officer grabbed her and wrapped a towel he found hanging on the door knob around her.

"Ma'am, can you tell me what happened here?"

Kelly looked at the police officer and heard him, but nothing he was saying was making sense. She watched as the second officer cuffed and dragged Theron out the door. Her tears were burning her cheeks as they rolled down her face.

"I'm sorry. What did you ask me?"

"I need to know what happened here."

"Um, I really don't know, officer. I woke up because I heard Chimere screaming." Kelly sat on the end of Chimere's bed and put her head in her hands. "We went to a party last night, and I had a little too much to drink. I don't know, I don't know."

The officer placed what he hoped was a comforting hand on her shoulder. "It's all right now. Your friend is going to be fine. The ambulance will be taking her to Grady Memorial. Do you think you can pull it together and go put some clothes on? I can give you ride if you'd like."

"No, it's okay. I need to shower. I'll get there. Thank you, officer...?"

"My apologies, I'm Officer Lucas. Are you sure you're okay?" The officer handed her a card as she nodded in the affirmative. "Alright, here is the police report number. My number is on the back if you have any questions."

Kelly looked at the letters and they were all a blur. "Oh, the blood is not mine. It's all Theron's. Yeah, okay, thank you again, Officer Lucas."

"You better give your landlord a call to come fix your front door."

Kelly pulled the towel tightly around her, followed the officers to the door, and shook her head. "Yes, yes, I will do that right now."

"You should get a call from the DA in a couple of days to let you know the trial date and if you both need to show up. Just keep the case number handy. If you haven't heard from someone by the end of the week, give me a call."

Kelly stood in the open door watching the police leave. She noticed a couple of her neighbors staring at her, and she realized she was still draped in only a towel. She waved and closed the door as best she could. She grabbed the phone and was dialing when there was a knock on the half-closed door. When she opened it, she was glad to see the smiling face of their landlord Mr. Woodward with his tool box.

"Oh, Mr. Woodward, I'm so sorry. He was beating her up. He was hurting Chi-Chi. I'm sorry"

He took one look at Kelly, reached out, and hugged her. "It's okay, baby girl, it's okay." He stood there and held her as she cried. "Let me go get the missus to help you clean up in here."

"He was hurting Chi-Chi. I don't know what happened, Mr. Woodward. Why? Why did he do this? Oh my God, why?" She looked at the door and then at Mr. Woodward. "No, I have to get to the hospital. I can clean this mess when I get back. Thank you, Mr. Woodward. Thank you so much."

"Kelly, you and Chimere are like me and Mrs. W's daughters. This ain't no problem. Okay, now you gon' get yourself together while I fix this door. Come on by after you seen Chimere and give us an update, you hear me?"

Kelly hugged Mr. Woodward and ran to the shower. When she stepped into the living room, the door looked brand-new. Although she felt refreshed after the shower, her head was pounding and her stomach was feeling queasy. She grabbed a Coke out of the fridge and took four Tylenols. She threw on jeans and an AKA T-shirt, called Jumbo, and filled him in with as much detail as she could before she broke down sobbing. He agreed it would be better for him to drive.

While she was waiting for Jumbo, she had tears running down her cheeks. She packed a few things for Chimere. She sat on her friend's bed and cried. She thought, *Why didn't I hear the door? Why didn't I get here sooner?* The knock at the door made her jump. When she looked through the peephole and saw Jumbo's face, she quickly opened it and jumped in his arms.

"It's okay, Kel. Come on, baby. Let's get to the hospital. Did you call her parents? Good thing they arrested Theron, because once the brothers find out, I wouldn't want to be in his shoes right now."

"Yeah, they took his trifling bleeding butt in handcuffs. Oh God, no! I can't call her father and tell him this. He would be on the next thing smoking and in jail for murder.

34

You know Chi-Chi is her daddy's baby! What would I tell them? I don't even know what happened myself. Let's go."

Jumbo chuckled. "Girl, I can just imagine your itty-bitty self beating him with that book. Sorry, Kelly, but that is an image I wished I had on video."

They got in the car and raced to Grady Memorial. The hospital was busy and crowded. Kelly made her way to the information desk and was told which room Chimere had been moved to. They headed toward the elevator and up to the room. Kelly froze when she opened the door and saw her friend lying on a bed with an IV tube, bandages, and bruises all over her swollen face. She grabbed Jumbo's arm.

"I can't go in there! I just can't. Oh God, I'm so sorry! Her dad is going to be so mad at me. I promised I would look out for her." She was wide-eyed and on the verge of hysterics, tightly clutching Jumbo's jacket. "He is going to kill me!"

"Baby, come on now. He's not going to kill you. This is not your fault. You stopped this from being worse than it is. He'll just be glad his daughter is alive. Now what he'll do if he catches Theron—"

"He can't find out! Please don't tell my daddy!" Chimere's voice groggy and muffled with her mouth barely able to open.

They both started when they heard Chimere's weak voice. Kelly ran to her bed and laid her head on her friend's chest. Chimere winced as she stroked Kelly's head to comfort her. Jumbo leaned over and kissed Chimere on the only unbruised spot of her face; a single tear rolling down his cheek. Chimere reached out and grabbed his hand.

Fighting back the tears, Jumbo whispered, "Chi-Chi, I'm so sorry. What happened?"

Jumbo moved to the end of the bed to crank up the head to help Chimere sit up a little better. He found two chairs and pulled them to her bedside. She told them the details as best she could before she broke down and began to cry hysterically. The time went by quickly as Chimere retold the events that led to Theron breaking down their door, losing control and beating her. By the end of her story, Kelly had climbed into the bed and was holding her friend as tightly as she could without causing her more pain. Chimere begged them not to tell her dad. At least, not until after she was healed.

The more Chimere spoke, the angrier she got. Kelly tried to calm her friend down with a change of subject or make her laugh. It was at a point of laughter when they were interrupted by Officer Lucas.

Chimere noticed them first as they came into the room. Because she had been unconscious until she arrived at the hospital, she had no idea they were the police from the apartment. Kelly's smile let her know they were not strangers.

Kelly stood to extended her hand to the officer. "Hello again, Officer Lucas. This is my boyfriend, Jim Smalls. He drove me here. I wouldn't have made it here in the state of mind I was in. How much damage did I do to that creep?"

"Hello again, Miss Hope." Officer Lucas firmly shook her hand. "Glad you made it here in one piece, you had me a little worried. Mr. Smalls, glad you were available to help these young ladies out. Well, Miss Royle, good to hear you're laughing. Miss Royle, I'm Officer Lucas. I was at your apartment this morning. I hate to bother you here, but I have to get some information from you. Is that okay? Do you feel up to answering a few questions?"

"Um, sure. I was just filling Kelly and Jumbo in on what happened. I just found out what my girl did." Chimere stopped as tears streamed down her face. "It seems I owe her my life for real now. We've been friends since second grade, and she's always been there for me, one way or another. I'd be lost without her."

"Yes, Miss Hope did a number on Mr. Dunkle. Besides a mild concussion and a broken nose, he had to get twenty-two stitches across his face. That will leave a nasty scar. Now just take your time, and if you need to take a break, let me know, all right? I do want to let you know we have filled out the preliminary paperwork for an order of protection for you against Mr. Dunkle. He will remain in custody until his bond hearing, which is currently set for Monday, July 29 at 9:00 a.m. That should give you enough time to heal. We got plenty of photos while you were unconscious, so don't worry about the judge seeing how badly he hurt you. Miss Hope and Mr. Smalls, could you please excuse us?"

Kelly hugged her friend while Jim kissed her on her forehead, and they left the room, closing the door behind them. Officer Lucas sat in one of the chairs and pulled out his notebook. He sat silently reviewing his notes. His partner, Officer Dumonte was wearing a Canon 35mm camera around her neck, came and stood on the other side of the bed. Officer Lucas pulled a small cassette recorder from his pocket.

"Miss Royle, I have to ask you some questions. Miss Hope wasn't sure on the details. Mr. Dunkle wasn't very talkative. We need to get a few more photographs now that you are awake, and I need your permission to record. Is it all right with you if we record?"

"Oh, sure, that will be fine. Officer Lucas, you didn't contact my parents, did you? I want to be the one to tell them…but not just yet." Chimere became visibly agitated. "My—my Dad is not a man who will pause for an explanation. He will come here specifically to do serious bodily harm to Theron." Chimere's hands were clenched on the stiff hospital sheets. "Oh, I don't even want to think about what this will do to my mom."

"No, Miss Royle, we didn't contact your parents. Miss Hope already told us it would be wiser to let you girls handle informing them. Shall we get started? We don't want to keep you since you should really get your rest. Please speak as clearly as possible." He switched on the recorder and began to speak. "Sunday, June 9, 1985, 12:45 p.m. at Grady Memorial Hospital with Miss Chimere Royle. An incident occurred approximately 8:30 a.m. at Miss Royle and Miss Hope's apartment. Miss Royle, have you been given any sedatives or pain medications? Miss Royle, how do you know the assailant, Mr. Dunkle?"

"No, not since I arrived. They gave me a couple of aspirin for the pain. They want to keep an eye on me to ensure the effects of my concussion subside. I met Theron—I mean, Mr. Dunkle in my sophomore year at a fraternity-sorority mixer."

"All right, so you two were dating?"

Chimere winched in pain as she sat up and wildly shook her head from left to right. "No, sir. Actually, we were just friends. Sometimes we would study together. There were a few times over the last few years we would grab a bite to eat or maybe watch a movie here and there. I wouldn't say we dated, and I made it clear to Ther—I mean, Mr. Dunkle—that I wasn't interested in a relationship."

"Did you ever have a physical relationship with Mr. Dunkle?"

"No, sir!" Chimere sat up as straight as she could, her face flushed. "Um…I am still a virgin, sir. My parents are very strict. I believe in honoring my parents and the way they raised me."

Officer Lucas looked at her and then up at Officer Dumonte with raised eyebrows.

"Sir, I know it is hard to believe, but my mom always told me I'm a treasure—not to be given away, but earned and cherished by the right man. The man who is worthy of enjoying the treasure must be a man of character. One who will respect I have kept the treasure secure until it is presented to him. And it will only be presented to him on the day of our marriage. College is where we spread our wings, sometimes keeping them stretched a little too much after leaving the nest. Admittedly, I've singed my wings a few times in my four years here, but none of which included sex."

Officer Lucas smiled, reached out, and patted Chimere's hand. "Very good, Miss Royle. That is commendable! Were you aware Mr. Dunkle had romantic feelings toward you? Was this the first time he became violent?"

"Honestly, Officer Lucas, I knew he liked me. I explained the day we met I didn't believe in premarital sex and friendship was the best he could hope for. I came here determined to achieve the goals I had set for myself. We studied together sometimes, usually with several others. Never has there been a romantic moment, nor did I ever give him any signs of that happening." Chimere hesitated, and the tears returned. Replaying the time spent with Theron, she tried to think if she had missed signs that he would be this brutal. "Never, ever did I have any inkling that he would snap like this. We've been friends for almost three years, and he's seen other men trying to talk to me."

Tearfully, Chimere recounted the events of the last two days. After about thirty minutes, Officer Dumonte looked at Officer Lucas. Officer Lucas stood, tapped Chimere on her shoulder, then went to stand at the door. Officer Dumonte took a few more photographs as a cue to her partner it was over. She reached down and squeezed Chimere's hand tightly.

"Miss Royle, that's enough for now. Thank you so much. You did good sweetie. Sorry to make you do this now, but you will need to tell this one more time in court. Officer Lucas or I will be there for the entire trial." She leaned closer and whispered. "I applaud your parents and you for holding true to how they raised you. We will be back in touch if we have any more questions. You take care and get yourself better now." She squeezed Chimere's hand. "Oh, and Miss Royle, make sure you get to the department to sign the paperwork for the order of protection. It would be best to have the order in place before we go to court."

Officer Lucas waited until Officer Dumonte had left the room. "Miss Royle, I don't normally do this, but I feel compelled to share something with you before I leave. I hope you can find it in your heart to forgive Mr. Dunkle. He was very distraught and remorseful. All he kept repeating was how truly sorry he was for hurting you. I understand you are hurting right now, but the pain will subside soon and the injuries will heal."

He then he walked back to her bedside. "I get the feeling you are a very strong young lady. You're going to be just fine. I know it won't be easy while you're hurting, but please hear me out. I'm not saying you have to do it today, but please search your heart and forgive this young man. I ask that you this do this for you. I'll be praying for you." He gave her shoulder another squeeze before he pulled out a card, flipped it over, and scribbled something on the back. "This is my card. I put my direct line on it. Call me anytime if you need anything. Good-bye, Miss Royle."

Through tear-filled eyes, Chimere looked at the card then at Officer Lucas. She wanted to speak, but the words were jumbled in her head. She wanted to hug him for going the extra mile for her, but she was still in too much pain. All she was able to get out was a weak thank you as he exited the room. No sooner had the door closed that it flew opened again with Kelly racing to her side.

Kelly slid behind her in the bed and started to braid her hair. "Gee-whiz, they were in here forever! So what did they tell you?"

"Kel, can we not talk about it right now? I just want to try to forget everything."

"Oh, sweetie! I'm sorry. Sure. Sit back and let me finish these braids, so you don't look like a troll doll."

They giggled as Kelly gently braided her thick hair.

Looks Like We Made It

A very light coat of makeup was just enough to mask the faded facial bruising on graduation day. The chiffon sleeves of her white dress camouflaged the still-dark bruises there. Chimere knew she would eventually have to tell her parents, but she didn't want to sully this most important day of her life. It saddened and angered her that Theron wasn't going to be able to see her walk across the stage.

Every day, the words of Officer Lucas kept playing over in her mind. She gazed in the mirror trying to feel forgiveness for Theron in her heart. She almost felt like she had…until she moved. Any wrong move resulted in searing pain in her mending ribs. The left side of her face throbbed when she lied down. She moved in closer to the mirror.

"You will get there, because it's not worth holding on to this anger. You will have to work on getting there, but not today. You and Kelly had prepared for this day for too long. Right this minute, it's all about you girlfriend. You did the dang thang. Skee-wee!"

"Skee-wee! Yes, we did this." Kelly came to stand at her side.

They smiled as they looked in the mirror. Chimere turned to her friend put a strand of hair in place and kissed her cheek. They locked arms and smiled as they made their way to the next phase of their journey. Waiting for them when they arrived were Chimere's parents, Rayner and Amara and her younger sister, Samara.

A few moments later, walking proudly was Kelly's mother, Alice and her older brother, Kevin. Kelly mustered up her best smile as they posed for the pictures to commemorate this triumphant day. Both mothers had already begun to cry.

Her father hugged her mother proudly, yet his focus was on his eldest daughter and her best friend. He was proud of both his girls. He often teased them about being joined at the hip since they were together so often. They had proved they could be trusted, and he was glad they chose to go away from home together. He spent much of their first year nearby, but after a few months, he left at peace with the thought that they were fine. Mr. Woodward promised to keep a close eye on them.

The moment was nearing, and the girls needed to be in place with their caps and gowns. More tears were shed as everyone hugged, kissed, and parted ways. Chimere and Kelly grabbed hands and headed inside when Chimere stopped because someone called her name. She glanced at Kelly, who was grinning, then she followed her line of sight. Approaching them with large beautiful floral arrangements was Medan. He hugged them both and kissed Chimere on the cheek. Gently but firmly, he held Chimere's hand.

"Well, this is such a great day. I'm proud of two of my favorite AKAs! You guys look fantastic."

They laughed, but Medan and Chimere's eyes were locked tighter than a padlock on a chain. In unison, Kelly and Chimere thanked him and then left him standing at the entry. They locked arms and made their way to the holding area.

The air was filled with excitement and sorority calls were escalating as the area filled with Spelman's graduating class of 1985. The Dean of Students was passing out the honors collars, which caused even more screeches and sorority calls. The area was rumbling with eager anticipation for the young ladies ready to take their places in the world. The commencement began with uplifting speeches. A few alumni shared words of glee and promise of wondrous futures for this class of outstanding young women. As each name was called, the graduates made their way to accept the tangible proof of the accomplishments. The house boomed and the clamor of support was almost deafening as the graduates moved their tassels to the left. Tears of proud observers were shed as the graduates made their final salute of tossing the caps with a joyful shout.

Chimere was excited to see all of her sorority sisters in honors collars. For the first time in weeks, she actually felt happy. At this moment, she knew everything was going to be better. She made her rounds, taking photos of former classmates and the many friends she had made throughout the four years. Now the smile that graced her face was genuine, and all the feelings of remorse were dispelled with each embrace. Her parents had made reservations for them at Benihana's for a celebratory dinner later that evening. The families were staying at the new Downtown Marriot, so they agreed to meet there before, so they could all arrive together.

When they arrived at their apartment, the phone was ringing as the entered. Kelly got through the door first and snatched the phone so quickly the base fell to the floor. They looked at each other and laughed. Chimere made her way to the kitchen to find a vase for the roses and other bouquets they had received.

"Keke, proud Spelman graduate speaking." She laughed. "Oh, hey, Da'Man! Thanks again for the flowers. Chimere is putting them in water right now."

"Hey, KeKe, proud Spelman graduate. I couldn't find you guys afterward. I wanted to invite you both to a party at my house tonight."

"Cool, but we already have plans. Our folks are here so…"

"Well, you know how we do it. So come on by after you're done, if you want. Jumbo said he had plans. He is going with you all, right?"

"Now you know he is. My mother would knock his block off if he didn't." She laughed. "I'm surprised he didn't tell me about the party."

"Oh really? Well yeah, that is a little surprising. Well, I have to run a few more errands. Hope to see you all later. By the way, tell Chi-Chi not to bring her boyfriend."

Kelly was silent for a moment. She knew from his statement Medan didn't know about the incident. "Oh, you can bank on him not being there. He isn't her boyfriend anyway. He was more like a wannabe. Jumbo hasn't mentioned him to you has he?"

"Nah! Jumbo hasn't been around lately. He kept telling me he had to study and get ready for finals. Anyway, why would he talk to me about that joker? That dude and some of the other Alpha's he hangs with are complete idiots." He chuckled. "Not everyone can hang tough with us Que-Dogs!"

Chimere was sitting in their wicker throne chair, tapping her foot and motioning Kelly to tell her what Medan was saying.

Kelly waved her off and turned her attention back to Medan. "We'll try, but we're not going to promise. It's been a long three days, and we are a little tired."

"Yeah, I remember how hectic graduation week can be. Jumbo knows where my house is, so if you can, it'd be cool to see you ladies there."

"Cool! Talk to you later, Da'Man."

Kelly hung up and looked at her friend with a big grin." I am beginning to think someone has the hots for you."

"Oh, please Kelly. That man is not even thinking about me like that. So what did he want?"

"He wants us to come to his house for a party tonight. I told him we have family stuff to do and if we could, we'd be there. He told me to tell you not to bring—um…for you not to bring Theron. Jumbo hasn't said anything, so he doesn't know. I'm surprised though, 'cause it was the topic around campus for the last couple of weeks."

Chimere's eyes lit up, and she smiled. "He said that, really?"

"Actually, he said for you not to bring your boyfriend. Chi, girl, I'm telling you he has the hots for you. That's what you get for sitting on his lap at that party." They skee-wee in unison and laughed. "So, proud Spelman graduate, you want to go or what?"

Chimere took a deep breath and sighed. "Jumbo is such a good friend, but I'm glad he didn't tell him. You know they're frat brothers, and normally, information like that would be all over by now. I'm glad Theron is still in jail. I can only imagine what the Que-dogs would do to him." She took another deep breath. "It might be fun, so let's just see how we feel after dinner, okay?"

"You got it! I'm going to try to take a nap before we head downtown. Wake me up in about an hour. Cool?"

"Sure, no problem. I need to pack a couple more boxes for my parents to take back home. Plus, I need to get a few things ready for my job at the King Center. I'm so excited." She began to do her version of Walk like an Egyptian dance moves.

"Yeah, I can see that by this little fit here you are excited. I'm excited for you too. Really, I'm proud of you for wanting to make a difference and for accepting this job. I really thought the offer to be a senator's aid was going to be your choice."

"I thought I was going to get in deep with all the Washington bigwigs. But when you said you were going to stay here to teach, you know I wasn't going to leave you here all by your lonesome. What would you do without me?"

They laugh and hug each other tightly. Kelly trotted off to her room, leaving Chimere alone among the half-packed boxes scattered around the living room.

Chimere ambled around, peeking into and touching each box until she reached the patio door. The sounds of honking horns, various roars of triumph, and shouts of joy slammed her in face. She stepped out on to the patio to shouts of friends and former classmates calling out her name. The jubilant skee-wee of sorority sisters echoed through the air. This day would be etched in her mind as a bitter sweet one. A triumphant step to the beginning of her journey into independence and adulthood. For the first time since she left Indiana, she felt like a full-fledged adult. Up until their senior year, time seemed to be moving slower than the earth's rotation. Finally, she had succeeded in reaching one of her goals—the goal of getting a bachelor's degree she and Kelly had set for themselves in seventh grade.

She felt happiness mixed with sorrows at the ending of the best time of her life. The doorway was now wide open for all the possibilities that lay ahead. Her heart was heavy with sadness at the loss of friendship and the imprisonment of the one man she thought she could count on. Tears rolled down her cheeks as each memory flashed through her mind. This day was truly her induction into the ups and downs of life and feelings of bitter sweetness.

The westerly winds blew in the smells of barbeque and frying chicken. The gradual rise of the music began to dance through the air. Chimere stood watching the helter-skelter of bodies beneath her, all ready to celebrate spending one last night on youthful escapades and throwing all cautions to the wind with dancing and drinking until the police would come to quiet them down to a dull roar.

Trying to remember every face and all the actions, Chimere sat on the patio for a good thirty minutes.

Surprisingly, she managed to sit unnoticed as the beautiful summer breeze calmed her. At that time, not once did her mind carry her to the horrific moments in her closet. She glanced at her watch and decided she would try to get a short nap before they have more excitement at Benihana's.

Her bed was shaking as Chimere woke up to find Kelly jumping up and down above her.

"Eww! Keke, I don't want to see your cute pink panties!" Chimere laughed, putting her hands, fingers spread, over her face. Kelly stopped jumping and plopped down just as Chimere rolled out from under her. "KeKe, one of these days, I'm not gonna roll out fast enough and you're gonna smash me."

They laughed as Kelly lied down next to her. "So don't you think we need get our hind parts ready to go hang with the family? Chi, I know you hate getting all sentimental and stuff, but I need to tell you how much you mean to me. I know I never would have passed some of my classes if you hadn't been here to help me. We've been friends forever. The two of us being able to share this day is our dream. It's just…," Kelly hesitated with tears welling in her eyes. She struggled to continue. "I know we said we wouldn't talk about what happen, but I need you to know I would have killed that bastard! I'm so sorry I didn't get to you sooner. You know if I had lost you, I would have just died or Pops would have killed me!"

With tears streaming smearing her mascara, Chimere reached over and hugged Kelly. "I know, KeKe. I feel the same way about you. I'm grateful you were here." She wiped the tears from Kelly's face and then her own. She was silent for a moment and then suddenly she began to laugh. Kelly looked at her and started laughing with her. "I hate that I didn't see your half-naked, hungover butt beating him with my poli-sci book. Every time I think about that, I get the visual, and I can't help but laugh and be so proud of you for taking that risk. Theron was out of control, and we could have both ended up in the hospital…or worse."

They sat up and looked at their smudged makeup and laughed. Kelly held up her right arm and bent her the elbow with her fist up. Chimere smiled and did the same. Simultaneously, they bumped fist and crossed arms. They laughed as Kelly jumped up to leave.

As Kelly was walking to her room, she stopped and turned around. "Chimere, we will be AKAs for the rest of our lives and our call will always make us sorority sister, but our crossed fist makes us more. You know that, right?"

"Dang, Keke! Have you been drinking already or what? Where is all this mushy talk coming from? You are never this sentimental. What is going on?"

"Nothing. I guess the anticipation was so high and now it seems like a big letdown. I'm glad you decided to stay here with me. Okay, I'm all right now. Let's get ready and get out of here. Jumbo will be here in twenty minutes. You know he hates having to wait on one woman, let alone two women." She laughed as she skipped to the bathroom.

Jumbo was knocking on the door just as Chimere was hopping down the hallway and putting on her shoes. As soon as she opened the door, she grabbed him and hugged him tightly.

"Girl, you better get off me! You know I have a jealous girlfriend." Jumbo laughed as Chimere tightened her hold on him." Chi-Chi, girl, you are choking me. You okay?"

Chimere stopped, smoothed her clothes, and looked at Jumbo. "Sorry, Jumbo. I think some of Kelly's excess emotions rubbed off on me. So I hear Da'Man is throwing a party tonight. Are you going?"

He stopped and turned to look at her innocent face with a grin on his face. "Since when are you interested in an Omega party, especially of a former one with the reputation of being a player?" He gently shoved Chimere and started laughing. "Oh dang! You like Da'Man. So finally, Miss Goal-driven is letting down drawbridge, eh? I can't believe I missed that. So you got a *thing* for my brother, huh?"

"Jumbo, please get real. You are taking a simple question way too far. No, I don't have a *thing* for your brother. For your information, he brought Kelly and me roses. Since he couldn't find us after our graduation, he called here and invited us. I guess my real question should have been why *you* didn't mention it."

Jumbo placed a hand on her shoulder and looked at her sweet pretty face. He smiled and kissed her on the forehead. "So, Old Medan was at the graduation and brought flowers, huh?" He laughed. "I didn't mention it because family is in town. I knew we were going to be spending most of the evening with them. With all the stuff going on, I guess I figured y'all would be too tired to go to a party. So there was no need to mention it. Yeah, after I dropped you guys home, I plan to head out to Decatur." He shook her a little and chuckled. "Kelly, come on girl. We're gonna be late! I don't want your mom thinking I don't know how to be prompt."

Kelly came out of her room laughing and doing the cha-cha-cha. "Please, my mother knows I never get anywhere on time. You will be scoring some real brownie points by getting me to the hotel on time." She took baby steps to where Jumbo was standing. He grabbed her arm, then Chimere's arm.

They all laughed as they left the apartment. They arrived at the Marriot Marquis a little early. When they entered the lobby, it was evident in the décor that a massive amount of money went into this new downtown hotel.

Just as they were about to check at the front desk, Mr. Royle called out. In his day, Rayner "Ray" Royle was considered to be a very smooth, sophisticated man. Always professionally dressed, he was handsome with a short salt-and-pepper afro, dark coffee-brown complexion, and had an old–school, Shaft-type stroll. His height and his posture were distinguishing characteristics, which, in his time, were proof he was not a pimp or a hustler. His faced glowed with pride as he approached the three of them at the front desk.

"Daddy!" Chimere stepped back, gave her father an up-and-down look, and then a thumbs-up of approval. "All right now. Daddy, you are looking awfully dapper! You must be trying to catch some sexy woman tonight, huh?" She laughed as she saw her mother approaching.

"As long as it is the sexiest woman I've loved for over thirty years." Amara Royle stepped up and locked arms with her husband. He gently patted her hand and kissed her long on the cheek. "There you go, mission accomplished. I caught the only one for me."

"Oh, Daddy! You are so corny sometimes."

"Hush, Chimere. I love seeing and hearing how much your parents love each other. I only hope I will find a man to love me like that. Your folks have the kind of love that is once in a lifetime. Man, with the way things are going with our generation, it is getting hard just to find a man not all caught up in sports." Kelly nudges Jumbo, who was not prepared for it and stumbled a little. "I hope and pray the man I marry will be there when I'm old and saggy." Jumbo raised both hands in surrender.

They are all laugh when Kelly's mother, Alice, followed by Kevin and Samara, came to join them. The late afternoon Atlanta air was perfect for them to take a short walk to Benihana's. Chimere and Kelly were in the lead, both

55

walking backwards to make sure they missed none of the accolades being tossed out by their parents. Kelly would catch her brother frowning. She'd put her thumbs in her ears, wiggled her fingers, and stuck out her tongue at him, causing the group to burst into laughter.

They were seated at a table with another family who are celebrating a twenty-first birthday. Rayner ordered everyone of age Sake to toast to the occasions at the table. The evening was filled with laughter and stories of past childhood antics. The meal and conversation made time fly, and they were almost the last guests to leave. They walked back to the Marriot in silence and said their good-byes.

Rayner embraced his daughter and kissed the top of her head. "Baby, you know Daddy is only a phone call away if you need me. You can't see it, but my chest is so puffed out with pride right now. Momma and I knew you would do well. I'm so proud of you wanting to stay here in Atlanta, but if—"

"Dad, I'll be fine." Chimere grabbed her dad's hands and looked him straight in the eyes. "Kelly and I are good here. We take good care of each other. I know you worry, but really, I'm good. You and Momma taught me well, and whether you believe it or not, I was listening to every word. Plus, Jim is just around the corner. And if I ever need to come back, I know you and Momma will take me in without a question. Now y'all get some rest. See you in the morning when you come to get the boxes."

"Okay, kiddo, you win. Y'all be careful." He turned to Jumbo, placed one hand on his shoulder, and extended his other hand to shake. Jumbo stood up taller and firmly shook his hand. "Jim, take care of my girls! If anything happens to them, I will hold you responsible, you hear me?"

Jumbo shuddered, but he kept his eyes fixed directly on Rayner Royle. He wanted to tell him what had happened, but he had to keep his word to Chimere. He didn't want to let this man down, nor did he want to break the trust he had with Chimere and Kelly. He looked at the girls' anxious looks and smiled.

"Yes, sir! With my life."

"Very well then. Good-night kids."

Jumbo locked arms with the girls. They looked from one to the other and began singing "Ease on Down the Road" doing the dance from the Wiz all the way to the parking garage. Jumbo opened the doors for them, but they were still laughing so hard it was difficult to get in. Kelly had tears in her eyes from laughing.

"You guys, I don't want to go home yet." Kelly spoke in between giggles. "Jumbo, can we go to Da'Man's party for a little bit? It is just way too early to go home. After what we've accomplished, we deserve a little bit of party time."

"Yeah, Jumbo, let's go to the party for a little while. What can it hurt? We are almost halfway there, right?" chimed in Chimere.

Jumbo got in the car, started the engine, and revved it. "Y'all are spoiled rotten. Get in. Let's go." The girls shrieked with glee, *skee-wee*d, and jumped in the car.

The downtown streets were full of people walking around and enjoying the pleasant Atlanta evening. The feeling of joy rolled up and down the streets with many graduates from Spelman and Georgia State. As they entered I-85 heading to Decatur, traffic was inching slowly. Once they merged onto I-20 east, the flow picked up. They pulled up to Da'Man's street. It was packed with people and hardly had any place to park.

"Look, I'm going to let you guys out here and go find a parking spot. Da'Man's house is—well, the one with all the people on the lawn. Find Da'Man and let him know I'll be there as soon as I park."

"Okay." In unison Chimere and Kelly replied. They jumped out of the car and trotted up to the front door. When Kelly turned to look, Jumbo was still sitting there, so she waved him off. Once inside, the aroma of barbeque, beer, and marijuana wafted around the large living room.

Chimere was lost in all the amazing pieces of African art work covering several walls. She never would have imagined Da'Man to be a collector of such exquisite art forms. She immediately was drawn to the large black marble statue finely chiseled into a form of a man and woman embracing. As she looked at all the statues and beautiful photographs of African faces and landscapes, a new respect for Da'Man formed.

At the far end of the room, Da'Man was standing behind a large cherrywood bar, serving drinks to a couple of Deltas. She could tell from the body language the girls were flirting with him. The longer she watched him, the more she understood why so many girls wanted him. It was more than evident he was very good with words and very suave. Not only was he the proverbial tall dark handsome man with his nicely trimmed goatee, he was educated and had a very good job. Now she found out he was even a little cultured, his smile was more dazzling than she remembered. He stood behind the bar in a crisp white-collared shirt with the sleeves rolled up to his elbows. When he handed drinks to the girls his right forearm exposed his Omega brand.

She tried to look away when he looked up but instead, she just smiled. He motioned for them to come to the bar. She pulled Kelly by the sleeve to get her attention. Just as they reached the bar, Jumbo came in through the back patio door. They greeted each other in Omega fashion. The house was in an uproar with all the various fraternities and sororities sounding off.

At Da'Man's insistence, Jumbo took both girls by the hand and gave them a tour of the house. Chimere was in awe of the elegant yet masculine décor of the house. Every room had some form of either African art or tribute to Malcom X or Martin Luther King Jr. The two bedrooms were all coordinated with the rest of the house. Chimere was surprised at how clean and put-together it was.

When they got back to the bar, Da'Man was once again surrounded by woman flirting with him. Chimere took Kelly by the arm, and they went out to the patio.

"Kelly, I can't believe how beautiful this house is. I've never seen a man, other than my dad, be so neat and orderly. Do you know what his real name is?"

Kelly laughed. "So you *do* like him? His name is Medan Freeman. He graduated at the top of his class in 1982. He's an engineer at Georgia Power. He has been single for the last three years. He claims he doesn't have time to date. He thinks all the girls here are silly and immature. That's all I know. Jumbo told me all this after the—"

"Kelly, I only asked for his name!" Chimere rolled her eyes, walked away, and headed over to where a few of their sorority sisters were sitting by the pool. She joined them. Kelly went back inside, and as soon as she got to the bar, Da'Man refilled her a cup.

"Where'd your friend go that quick?" Medan asked looking around the room. "Has she even asked about me, Keke? So what is up with her and that guy anyway?"

"Oh, she's out there by the pool. I told you they were just friends. She is not interested in anyone—not even you, Da'Man. One thing I will tell you about my sister is she is very determined and focused. And honestly, you ain't got what it takes to get her unfocused."

"What in the world does she have to focus on? Y'all just graduated. I was there and saw it! Is she going for a master's or something?"

"No, she's getting ready to start working at the King Center, and she intends to be deputy director of that place in three years. You should really be asking her these questions. I've already told you too much."

"Aw, come on, KeKe. Don't be like that. You know you're my favorite li'l sister. I know the only reason she was on my lap that night was she was tipsy. I've asked around and watched her at some of the parties over the last couple of years, and she is not like most of these silly college girls."

"Well, I must say, that is a little freaky, but I guess it's cool. You have a keen sense of observation. You act like she's an untouchable or something. If you act right, I'm sure she'll talk to you. Just don't act like you all cool and superfly."

He turned to Jumbo. "Hey, man, take over for me here. So where is she, Keke?"

Kelly and Jumbo both laughed. Kelly pointed to the pool. They watched as Medan strolled out to the pool.

When he reached Chimere, he just stood there for a minute. *Okay, here goes nothing*.

The other girls, who were sitting with her, saw him and began to fawn all over him. Kelly laughed because she could tell he is trying to be casual and not rude to any of the girls.

He pulled a chair over and sat to the left of Chimere, trying to distance himself from the cluster of girls. He sat, listened, and laughed for a while. Then the topic changed to the next steps for each of the girls in the group. Many of them were seeking to further their education and had entered master's programs in Atlanta, Chicago, and Florida. A few were preparing to begin working in their field of study. Medan was impressed with these women sitting by his pool. He was glad to see young black women ready to take on the corporate world with bright-eyed ambition and expectation.

He casually placed his arm on the back of Chimere's chair and leaned over to whisper in her ear. "Can we go somewhere and talk?"

She turned to look at him and smiled. "If you want to talk to me, we can do it right here."

He looked at her and smiled. "Oh, so it's going to be like that. Well, ladies, I wish you all the best of luck in your future. Enjoy yourselves and stop by the bar when you need more libation." He got up and went back into the house.

Just as he got to the bar, a tall light-skinned pretty girl came and grabbed his arm. He smiled and flirted with her but watching Chimere out of the corner of his eye. He hoped she was watching but was disappointed. She had moved to the other side of the pool and was talking to a couple of his frat brothers.

Finally, the pretty girl moved on, and he joined Jumbo behind the bar. "Hey, man! What's the story with your friend, Chimere? Is she always so cold? Did I do something to offend her?"

Jumbo laughed. "Man, I have never seen you so strung up on a girl before. What is it about that skinny brown chick that has you all twisted up? You know the only reason she was so friendly last time was she had too much to drink. I told you she is a good girl. I've known her almost four years and have yet to see her really let her hair down. She's very focused and driven. I like that about her, and it helps keep my girl in line." He nudged Kelly. "Right, babe?" Kelly waved him off like she was swatting flies and kept talking the group of girls at the end of the bar. "See? I have her in line, and she's a musician." They laughed.

"Jumbo, she is just not like anyone I've met in the six years I've been down here. She's pretty and smart. She can even be a little feisty—or at least, when she's drinking."

"Well you certainly can't keep her drunk, that's for sure. Give her time. She'll warm up to you. She was super quiet when I first met her. I thought Chi hated me that first year. It was hard, because I fell for this Little Miss Hot Stuff the minute I saw her at the '81 Step Off." He nudged Kelly to give her drink. "She was a pledging, and I couldn't take my eyes off her. But that Chimere, she was a tough nut to crack. Now she is the sweetest, kindest person. It pisses me off what that jerk Theron did to her. Oh—I mean…hell!"

"Who's Theron? Oh! Is that the idiot who was trying to block at the party a while ago? Oh, don't start backpeddling now, Jumbo. What happened?"

"Man, these girls will kill me if I tell you." He looked over Medan's shoulder to make sure Chimere was not within earshot. "I promised, and you know Ques have to keep their word!"

"Yeah, but we're brothers. We don't keep no secrets."

"True, but my word has to come before our bond. Sorry, man. But don't worry, it's all under control."

The intro for Anita Baker's "Angel" began to play. A couple of Ques lifted Kelly up onto the end of the bar and she began belting out the song. People started inside as Kelly's vocals echoed through the house.

Chimere made her way to the bar. One thing she loved was hearing her best friend sing. She had the voice of an angel and made this song seemed so appropriate for her. She looked up at her friend and smiled as Kelly outsang Anita Baker, hitting every note and remaining on pitch.

Kelly sustained the last note well after the end of the song, and the crowd roared with excitement. Some even began screaming for an encore. Kelly took her bows gracefully and declined the invitations to sing more. She hopped from the bar, grabbed Chimere by the hand, and strolled to the other end of the bar.

"Barkeep, can we have two long islands please?" She winked at Jumbo and Da'Man with a Cheshire cat-smile across her face.

Da'Man walked over and gave her another round of applause. "Whoa, Kelly! Girl, I didn't know you had pipes like that. I may have to hire you for the next big party I throw. Girl, you are a phenom! Where did you learn to sing like that, and why are you hiding out here in Atlanta with a voice that big? Don't make me pay for a ticket to Hollywood for you to go to Motown."

They all laughed. "Thanks, Da'Man. I've been singing since I was able to talk. I love music and would much rather teach than be on a stage. You wouldn't be able to afford my party rates." Kelly giggled. "I'd rather share my gift with kids who will appreciate it more. Anyway, the music industry is a little too cutthroat for me."

"Well, you may just have to give me the brotherhood discount. I'm serious. I host my department's Christmas party every year, and I would really love to have you doing some soulful Christmas carols along with some R&B. What would you charge for three hours—with breaks, free food, and drinks, of course?"

She looked at him and smiled. "You're serious? Well, honestly, the only way I'll do it is if I can bring my bodyguard and ah…my…um…stylist."

Jumbo started laughing. "Man, you know who those are right?"

"Kelly, if you bring it anything like you did tonight, you name your price and we will have a date."

"How about that! I come to a party to celebrate my graduation and walk out with a gig to help pay a bill or two. So let's see, can you work with fifty bucks an hour?"

"Oh, heck yeah! Just tell me what equipment you'll need, and I will have you set up right by the fireplace in the living room. It's a small group, about twenty to thirty people max. This year the party is going to be on Saturday, December twenty-first. I would like you to perform from nine until midnight. My crew will be pooped out by midnight. How does that sound?"

Kelly looked at Chimere and Jumbo. "Let me get back to you next month. I need to be sure my team will be able to attend." Kelly giggled and winked at Chimere.

"So, Chi-Chi, do you have any surprising talents?" Medan asked sincerely. "If I had known your friend was so talented, I would have had y'all at some of my company parties."

"Sorry, what you see is what you get with me. I'm just a background kind of girl."

"Yeah, right. I'm pretty sure you are more than a background girl."

"Well, yes I am a background girl. I don't like all the hoopla and stuff. I feel like I can get more done if people aren't breathing down my back, especially with the type of work I want to get involved with. Being on the front lines is not for me. I'm more of an organizer and a planner than a woman of action."

"Oh, really now." He looked at her with a raised eyebrow. "So what type of work are you trying to get involved with?"

"You sure you really want to have this discussion at your party? It's not that interesting, and I would rather not get in to it tonight. Maybe some other time." Chimere smiled at Medan and turned to talk to another Omega, who had been trying to go out with her for a year. Chimere had already decided to let her hair down tonight, and having fun was top of her list. She danced with several of the brothers from Alpha, a few of the Kappas, and every other man that asked her, except Medan.

Even though Medan was a little upset by Chimere brushing him off, it made him happy to see her having a good time. As he watched her, it became even clearer that she was the one he wanted. She was the woman he could see himself settling down with.

Kelly came, stood next to him, linked arms, and laid her head on his muscular bicep. "Don't worry, Da'Man. She is not always like this. We have had an exciting day with family. Give her time. She'll ease up on you after a while."

"Yeah, if you say so. Jumbo was right, she's a tough cookie. I just don't understand why she acts like I'm a bad guy. It makes me wonder what Theron did to get next to her. He seemed to have the key to that armor she has locked."

The mention of Theron made Kelly cringe, but she laughed and squeezed his bicep. "You make her sound like an iron maiden. You're forgetting one thing. You have a heck of a reputation. Then you have to remember when she's seen you at parties, you've had some sleazy chick with you. So you have to let her see the man I know, the intelligent, sweet, and generous one. That playboy role you play, you need to let him go if you want my girl to warm up to you."

"No, it's more like *Taming of the Shrew*." They laughed. "Wait, I didn't hang out with sleazy chicks. Anyway, that was a couple of years ago. Can't a brother get a pass for cleaning up his act?" He went back to playing bartender and flirting with the circle of newly pledged Deltas. He heard Kelly loudly clear her throat. He looked at her shaking her head with a did-you-hear-what-I-just-said look on her face. He smiled, handed the girls their drinks, and moved on to the guys waiting to get a cup.

The DJ played "Walk Like an Egyptian," starting a massive rush to the dance area with shouts of "Party ova here" sporadically around the room. Rounding off the excitement, the alumni of Omegas took the floor to stomp it out to "Word Up!" producing a thunder of Greek calls.

Chimere came back to the bar out of breath, flushed, and with a light film of perspiration on her forehead. As she reached for a napkin, her hand brushed Medan's. The brassy beat of "I Didn't Mean to Turn You On" slid through the empty space between them.

"Hey, Ms. Chi-Chi, can I get you something to drink?"

She looked up at his sweet broad smile. She couldn't help notice how handsome and kind he looked in this light. He looked like he'd just stepped out of a barber's chair. His goatee was neatly trimmed, hugging his strong chin. For the first time, she took long hard look at Medan. Her foggy image of him from previous parties and the stories she had heard made her form a not-so-positive opinion of him. Tonight, however, all she could see was his sweet smile, bright friendly eyes, and handsome virile facial structure.

"Sure, I would love a cup of ice water."

"At your service." He handed her a cup of ice water and a few napkins, intentionally lingering his hand on top of hers. Smiling, she thanked him and moved to the other end where Kelly and Jumbo were bouncing to the beat of "Raspberry Beret"

"Hey, Keke, Jumbo! Y'all about ready to get out of here?"

Chimere found herself bouncing with them and snapping her fingers. Before she even realized it, Kelly had maneuvered them onto the dance floor. The high pitch of Prince's voice always got them going, even when they were at home cleaning or doing homework. Something about his timber made them go wild. Jumbo had gone to stand by the bar where he was speaking to Medan. They laughed as they watched the girls dancing about the floor, sexy and wildly, until the song ended. They came over breathing hard and laughing. It was then Kelly noticed the crowd had really thinned out, and most of the people outside had left. She looked at her watch and then at Jumbo.

"Why didn't you tell me it was after three in the morning?"

"Because you didn't ask me." Jumbo laughed. "Plus, you guys needed to have a little fun—especially Chimere. See, I did the right thing. Y'all had a good time, right?"

In unison, they giggled and responded that they had. They looked at each other and all they could do was laugh harder. This had been a day of great accomplishment, frivolity, and joy. Without a word, both girls hugged each other and began to cry. Jumbo was confused by this emotional outburst and looked to Medan, who was pouring four glasses of champagne.

"This is good, man, they are happy. Just go with it." He handed each of them a glass. "I would like to propose a toast. To two of Spelman's finest and brightest and the major impact they will have on the world in the coming decade!"

They clinked glasses and laughed as the DJ announced his last song of the night would be a slow one. As Freddy Jackson began to croon, Medan took Chimere by the hand and led her to the dance floor. Slowly, they swayed to "Rock Me Tonight." Medan held her loosely so she wouldn't try to bolt. Much to his surprise, she didn't seem to mind. She actually seemed to be enjoying being in his arms, he hoped.

When the record ended, Chimere didn't miss a beat in walking away from him. He stood in the middle of his living room floor, feeling as if a part of his flesh had been removed. He slowly walked back over to the bar. They said good-byes, and Medan began clearing up the empty cups scattered along the bar. He stopped and turned to see if she glanced back but was disappointed as he saw she was going out his front door.

EVEN WITH MY EYES CLOSED

The radio was blasting when Jumbo cranked the engine. The voice of a local minister was urging the listeners to turn their lives over to Christ. Jumbo quickly popped in the closest cassette tape and turned down the volume. Before they entered the highway, Kelly had leaned over and her breath had slowed, letting him know she had fallen asleep. He glanced in his rearview mirror to check on Chimere. She was wide awake and nodding her head to the beat of the music.

"Chi-Chi, you know Medan really likes you, right?"

"No he doesn't, Jim. He likes the challenge. He's not bit more interested in me than I am in how rocks are formed." She looked straight at him in the mirror. "Even if he did Jim, you know I'm not interested in getting into a relationship. I start my new job in a week and—"

"Chimere Royle, why do you keep making excuses? You have done this same song and dance since I met you. What is the real problem? What are you afraid of?"

"Ha! I'm not making excuses. I have my goals, and I can't afford any distractions. I have to stay focused. It's hard enough keeping up with my best friend. Kelly is a lot all by herself, and it's the only relationship I trust right about now. I know Kelly told you…um…you know I won't have sex before I'm married, right? So why would I get with some guy who is only after that?"

"Chimere, not all guys just want sex, you know! Look at me and Kelly. We were together for two years before I even asked her." He glanced in the mirror to see her reaction. "Oh, you didn't know Kelly and I waited, did you? You thought those nights I slept over we were bush-banging and belly-bumping?" They laughed. "My father always told me the right woman would be one that makes you wait on it, and if she's easily pushed into giving it up, she's not worth keeping." He stopped for a light and turned to face Chimere. "Chi-Chi, there are a few of us good guys out there, and Medan is one of them. I've known him for almost six years and—"

"Green light! Jim, really, can we talk about something else? If it is meant for us to get together, then we will. You trying to sell me on him now is not working, especially not at almost four in the morning!"

"Chi-Chi, I really do love you and Kelly. Y'all are some special ladies. I know Kelly told you already that I'm moving to Savannah next month for six months. I need you to take care of my baby while I'm over there. I got hired for the management position. The closest place to do the training is in Savannah. It was either there or Tennessee. I figured, they are both a couple of hours drive, but at least in Savannah, I'm still in the same state."

Chimere rested her head on the headrest of Kelly's seat. "Whoa, Jim, really? She didn't tell me, but I'm happy for you. You wanted the job, right? I wished I would have known. I'm so proud of you, Jim! I know I've never told you, but I think Kelly *did well* when she picked you. You are great boyfriend and a great friend. I'm glad you're around." Jumbo glanced at her and noticed she had tears in her eyes. "I'm really gonna miss you, Jim. You'll be here for the court date, right?"

"Oh, Chi-Chi! I will be here even if I have to walk back. There is no way I'd let you and Kelly go through this without me." He reached back and rubbed Chimere on the head. "You guys are strong enough, but I want everyone to think I'm the muscle for you two."

They laughed as they pulled off the exit toward home. The laughter woke Kelly.

"What are you two laughing at? Oh, dang! Was I snoring?"

They laughed even harder as Jim pulled the car to the curb in front of their apartment. The street was still full of activity as people were making their way home or on to the next party. Jim looked at the girls and shut off the engine. He opened the door, waited for Kelly to exit, then pulled the seat up so Chimere could climb out of the backseat. He walked the girls up to the apartment, kissed Chimere on the cheek, and waited for her to go in.

"Babe, I would stay, but I have to meet my frat in a few hours. You get your rest, and I'll give you a call when our community event is over." He took her face in his hands. "Kelly, talk to Chimere. I think she'll listen to you more than she'll listen to me."

With furrowed eyebrows, Kelly asked, "Talk to her about what? Jim, you know as well as I do that Chimere is single-minded. Once she has set her goals, she sticks to them no matter what. Plus, with what Theron did, I think it is going to be a long time before she lets any man get close again." She smiled and kissed him on lightly on the lips. "I have enough of my own stuff to deal with. My man is leaving me for six months, and I'm going to miss him like nobody's business. I don't know how I'm gonna function. Chimere is a big girl and can take care of her own matters of the heart." She wrapped her arms around his neck and kissed him passionately. "Good-night—I mean, morning, my knight in purple-and-gold armor. I love you, Jim Smalls"

"I love you too, babycakes! You are my best girl, and I will love you forever!" He pulled her close and kissed all over her face, making his way to her lips. He lightly kissed her then patted her on the butt.

Kelly watched as he skipped down the stairs, whistling. She closed up, locked the door, and headed to Chimere's room. Chimere was sitting on the end of her bed, reading her employee pamphlet from the King Center. She didn't stir when Kelly came to sit next to her at the end of the bed. She put her arm around her, and Chimere leaned her head on her friend's shoulder.

"Kelly, can you believe it? We are college graduates! Remember when we were hiding from our moms in that stupid tent made out of my pink popcorn bedspread in my room? I know we had big dreams, lots of determination, and great expectations. We had talked big, but look at us now, graduated with honors and about to start working at the jobs we wanted. It's like the good luck fairy is smiling on us!"

Kelly laughed as they lay back onto the bed. "Good luck fairy! Where did you get that one? This ain't got nothing to do with no good luck fairy. We worked hard and earned them degrees. I'm thankful we've only had one black cloud on our years away from home. Are you ready to go to court? Are you ready to see him again?"

"Hmm…are you sure you graduated or has the south finally rubbed off on you?" Chimere sat up and looked at her. "Yes, I'm ready for this all to be over, so I can just go do my job and make a difference in someone's life."

"Silly, you're already making a difference in my life. That's enough." She laughed and sat up to put her arm around her friend's shoulder. "I'm proud of you, Chimere Latisse Royle!"

"Oh no, you didn't, Kelly Jean Hope!"

They fell back on the bed laughing. They laughed for a few minutes, then Kelly slapped Chimere on the thigh, got up, and headed to her room. She stopped at the door.

"Chimere, I love you, girl! I really do appreciate you not taking that job in Washington. I would have been lost without you here. Night!"

"Yeah, right! With Jim here, you wouldn't have been lost too long. I don't want to get all emotional, but you know I owe you my life. I'm glad Dad agreed to you being here. You know, if you had gone to a different college, I would have had to go to Indiana State or somewhere close to home. Thanks for always being there for me too! Love you silly. Good–night, Kelly!"

Kelly blew her a kiss and closed the door. She got to her room slowly, closing the door with her back, and stood there for minute. The tears came without warning.

There was a sudden flash of memory from that morning when she saw her best friend lying crumpled up on the floor, barely breathing. If Chimere had not been her tutor for all her literature classes, she would never had made it through with honors. She knew her voice made it easy in the musical and drama courses, but the truth was that Chimere was book smart.

What a momentous day this was for them all. Being the first of her family to have made it this far made it more joyous for her family. Although her mother would have preferred she got a more useful degree, her goal now was to be the best teacher she could be. She had made it through taking on part-time jobs to cover expenses when things were tight for her mom. She was grateful for Chimere and their friendship.

The Royle family was as close to millionaires as Kelly knew she'd get. Mr. Royle made an agreement with her and Chimere to pay for their apartment, utilities, car insurance, monthly gasoline allowance, and most of the food. Kelly's contribution was to keep Chimere safe. Now she was faced with keeping a secret from the only father figure she had, the one man who saw in her what even her own mother missed. Every day since, she had fought to keep her mouth closed and remain loyal to her first and best friend. Keeping her promise to Chimere was important to her. On some days, being torn by which allegiance was most important was more than she could bear.

With tears in her eyes, Chimere was looking at her naked body in the new full-length mirror she had hung behind her door. The bruises were mostly visibly gone, but the mental scars lingered like the smell of a skunk hit by a car. The headaches were coming more frequently, and her stomach was hurting from all the aspirin she had been taking. She was afraid to tell Kelly she was frequently experiencing short moments of blackouts. She wished the flashbacks and the memories would stop, but every time she closed her eyes, she could see the frighteningly angry face of Theron and his fist coming at her. She was glad finals were over, and she could try to give her mind a rest. She hoped the new job wouldn't be very mentally draining, because she needed to find some peace.

Fear kept her from telling anyone about the dreams she was having about the children, especially when she found out the boys were murdered in Atlanta a few years back. The dreams were surprisingly peaceful and pleasant. All the boys were playing when she would find them in a room of a house she was exploring. The house was always the same, and the rooms were all blue and calm. All she could do was hope the dreams would end. She knew telling anyone what the boys said to her would end up with her in Georgia Regional. She would try to stay awake as long as possible to keep from dreaming about the faces of the boys and young men who were once front-page news. In her dreams, they were happy. None of them ever spoke of pain, just how wonderful this place was they were in.

When the dreams became more frequent, she began to keep a journal. She had pages of dialog and information. The names of the boys were etched in her mind when she would go to the library to verify. Every one of them seemed so real, and their touch gave her such peace. They were always leaving her with a simple request. "Please tell my mom or grandma that I'm in a good place!" But none of them were clear on what had happened to them. All they would tell her is they couldn't remember the face of man that killed them, just the roughness of his hands on their necks. They all remembered the smell of strong liquor and cigars.

Often, after waking from the dreams, her bedding would be drenched with sweat. She would wake up freezing yet a sense of peace would come to her from spending time with the boys, whose sweet souls cried out to her. The first one named Eddie came to her while she was in the hospital, but she brushed it off as an effect of the pain medication. The next night, Eddie had brought with him two friends, Alfred and Milton. The similarities she noticed about the boys: they were young, had a dark black ring around their necks, blue lips, and were clothed in white. When she asked them about the marks, they would laugh and tell her she was being silly. They said they had no marks. The boys repeatedly requested to relay a message to their families or their loved ones.

Her grandmother had always told her that to dream about the dead just meant that they were watching over you. She had no fear of the dreams. However, their intention was to get a message to loved ones that everything was all right. These dreams were more like visions, because she was aware she was dreaming. She would tell the boys she knew they were dead and she was dreaming.

Eddie was always the cheerful leader. He was dancing his way to her with the other boys, so she could get their story. Each one told a different version. The only thing they had in common was the roughness of the hands that were grabbing them. The darkness was quickly chased away by a peace-giving light. They each spoke of the dark place and a raspy voice telling them they were not worth the air they breathed. The last night, Eddie came, and he brought with him three girls who told her the same story. They were snatched, drugged, woke up in a dark damp room, and the raspy voice telling them they weren't worth the air they breathed. The oldest of the girls did tell her the voice was a man, but the other person in the room with them was a woman. She knew it because before she felt peace, the scent of Jean Naté burned in her nostrils—the fragrance her grandma wore.

Someone Turn Off
the Darkness

Eddie came to her nightly, sharing more about the place he was in with the others. Not wanting to alarm friends or family, Chimere decided to seek out a medium, hoping once she shared the stories, she would be free from the burden of meeting with the ghost.

She went to Georgia University Student Union, hoping to find a posting of some sort. She looked through the personal ads in college periodicals and checked the bulletin boards of the local libraries and the local small newspapers. All led to dead ends or frauds. The fast pace of the office allowed her to find a little peace from the visions or dreams.

She entered the breakroom for an afternoon pick-me-up coffee. Two coworkers, Liby and Randella, were standing at the end of the counter, discussing a party they'd gone to where a past-life psychic gave readings. She approached the women as casually as she could.

"Hi, Liby! Hey, Randella! Did I hear you right, you went to a psychic? You guys don't believe in all that psychic stuff do you? Aren't they like people who practice voodoo and witchcraft?"

They all laughed. Randella look at Liby and answered for them both. "No, all mediums don't do witchcraft. You know voodoo is actually a religion, and you have to believe in it for it to work, right? My understandin' is that witchcraft is pretty close to voodoo in casting spells and stuff. I'm tellin' you this woman was *da bomb*! She didn't even use none of them tarot cards. She told me I was a duchess in the court of Henry the eighth and a concubine of King Tut." She stopped and looked at Liby, who had been nodding to affirm every detail. "The lives and stories are really connected with some stuff happenin' right now. Then she interpreted this guy's dreams. I mean, I'm not easy to get over on, but this woman—" She stopped, cleared her throat, and threw an Oreo cookie in her mouth.

"Well, it sounds really interesting. So where did you see this woman?"

Without even chewing, the Oreo was gone. Randella was getting visibly excited. "Oh, it was at a party at Liby's auntie over the weekend. She gave me so much hope for the future. We gonna see her for a private session, you wanna come?"

Chimere's eyes widened and she gasped. "I don't know… um…let me get back to you. When are you going?"

"Our appointment is tonight at six-thirty. We could all ride together, if you don't mind leavin' your car here at work. You know, Liby and I ride to work together. I'll drop you back off after the session or you can come and hang out with us. I'll get you back to your car," Randella said in between sips from a can of diet root beer.

Chimere walked over to pour herself a cup of coffee. When she looked up, Liby and Randella were staring at her, waiting for her answer. She giggled and smiled at them. "Sure, I'll come hang out. I don't believe in all that stuff, but I do find it interesting to watch. I will have to finish my week's end reports, so you might have to give me about fifteen minutes after work."

"Oh, that's no problem. We never get out of here right at five, no ways. Meet us out by my car at about five-thirty. That'll give us all enough time to clear up Friday's stuff," Randella suggested after swallowing another Oreo.

"All right, sounds like a plan. You ladies have a productive afternoon. I'll meet you at the five-thirty. I better get back to my desk. Those reports aren't going to write themselves."

"Yeah, I know what you mean. My receipts don't jump in no file drawers by themself neither. We'll see you later then." Randella nudged Liby to get out of the refrigerator.

Chimere could hear Randella's horse laughter as she stepped into her office. She had never hung out with any of her coworkers other than the introduction luncheon when she started. The climate in the office could be considered casual professional. She really didn't interact with Liby and Randella much unless she was submitting a project budget. She was wondering if she had made the right decision to go with Randella and Liby. During the last several months, she had been so focused on learning procedures and learning the community, she hadn't noticed anything about any of her coworkers. The hope to have the burden lifted was greater than any excuse she could tell herself. She needed to take a risk.

Kelly had been so distracted with the wedding planning, their soror's night outs were few. She enjoyed the pleasant distraction and attention of Medan. He had been around enough, so he knew many of the right people to expose her to. Her favorite was a private party of the Mayor, Andrew Young's, which gained her entrance into the circles of movers and shakers. Friday's at the office were pretty hectic with everyone trying to tie up loose ends before the weekend.

Liby stopped by her office to make sure she was still going to meet later. She glanced first at her watch, then at the pile on her desk, and reassured Liby she would be at the car by five-thirty. The minutes ticked by slowly, it seemed. She was growing more anxious as she completed the last weekly report. She hurriedly gathered her purse and other items at five-twenty. When Chimere arrived, Liby was sitting in the car playing with the radio, while Randella was rummaging through her trunk. She climbed in the backseat and leaned her head back.

Liby looked at her and laughed. "Yeah, girl, it was one of those Friday's in our department too."

They laughed as Randella jumped in, throwing a flask and some cups in the front seat. "What y'all laughing at?" She settled into her seat, adjusted her mirrors, and turned the ignition. "Ain't that far from here. So if traffic ain't too bad, we be there in about twenty minutes."

Chimere was getting comfortable in the backseat. Liby was in the front pouring the drinks. She handed Randella her cup and then passed one back to Chimere. Chimere sniffed the cup and knew she would hold the cup until they arrived.

The house was located on a very dreary street lined with a multitude of trees. The street was closed off to any aerial view. The overgrown dogwoods and magnolia trees in the dim light of sunset gave an eerie feel. As they pulled up the long driveway, the trees along the path formed a flowery arch. The only visible light emanated from a blinking street lamp. A slightly cool breeze picked up as soon as Chimere stepped out of the car, sending a chill down her back and causing her to shiver.

Randella giggled, and Liby smiled at her as she asked, "You okay there, little lady?" Randella and Liby laughed, as they made their way up the creaky stairs to a porch decorated with various wind chimes and mirrors.

The door was painted a very deep blue with a pentagram around a peephole. They knocked on the door and backed up a little as the door creaked menacingly open to a candlelit entryway filled with dark drapes and love beads, which led to various rooms. The décor was a mishmash of astrological symbols from framed and enlarged tarot cards to tie-dyed panels. The brightest color to be found in the entry were from bloodred beads covering the end of the entry way. Everything in the house told Chimere to turn around and run like crazy.

Just as she took a step backwards, the door slammed shut. The room was filled with aromas of clove, lavender, and sage. The deep midnight-blue curtains slowly parted, revealing a windowless candlelit room with a dark oval marble table and six high-backed chairs. From the shadows, a tall dark-clothed figured emerged, holding a deck of cards in one hand and smoking a clove cigarette from an orange glowing holder with the other. The three of them stood frozen, clutching each other. Chimere was in the middle of her coworkers. She took a step closer to the dark figure. Before she could take another step though, the figure moved into the light. Her face and large gray eyes seemed to glow. Her hands were boney and wrinkled with gold rings on every finger. Her nails were filed to a point, making them appear to be as sharp as daggers and coated in an eerie neon blue polish. She was dressed in an indigo caftan with matching turban that was embellished with emerald-green, sapphire-blue, and garnet-red crystals.

With an outstretched hand and a heavy accent, Madame Ulda invited the women to take a seat. "Welcome to Madame Ulda's, ladies. Please come into my parlor and make yourselves comfortable. I need you all to take a deep breath, relax, and clear your minds from all the cares of this day. Please, no matter what, I need you all to keep your palms on the table."

The room was quiet. Suddenly, Madame Ulda began to shake jerkily, accompanied by strange moans and groans. The candles flickered, but there was no breeze. Liby and Randella were awestruck, trying to keep their hands on the table as directed. Chimere was holding back laughter.

Madame Ulda stopped moving, opened her eyes wide, and stared directly at Chimere. "They are coming to you because they were told they could trust you. You know you have a very special gift, and this gift is not to be taken lightly. You are a very blessed young lady, and God will be using you more in time. Don't be afraid of this nightly visitor—or I should say, visitors. You must make sure to share the messages they give you. It is very important for you to tell their message. It will save someone's life!"

Madame Ulda slumped on to the table. A light breeze swept the room, blowing out all the candles. Liby let out a yelp. Just as suddenly, Madame Ulda sat up, reaching for the matches in the center of the table, and relit all the candles. Her eyes were bloodshot and seemed to change from gray to black.

"All right, ladies, let's begin with any questions you have for the spirits. They are very anxious to speak to you." She turned to face Randella and pointed a long, wrinkled finger at her. "There is a young man here, and he said to stop putting flowers at his gravesite. He wants you to take them to his daughter. She needs to be cheered up. He wants you to tell her he loves her and is very proud of her. Do you know who this young man is?"

Randella was on the edge of her chair with her mouth open but unable to speak, so she nodded her head for yes. She wanted to bolt out of the room and out of the house, but she couldn't seem to move her legs. She was shivering as Madame Ulda continued to speak to her. She slid her hand to cover Liby's as she spoke to her about a past reincarnation as a pioneer woman.

She told her of the deep soulful love that was coming her way. Madame took a deep breath and let it out slowly. She advised Liby to stop dabbling with white magic.

The issues she was trying to rid herself of with the white magic could easily be cured with forgiveness. Once again, Madame Ulda collapsed on the table. They looked at one another, not sure if that meant the end of the session. After a few more seconds, Chimere started to get up.

With her head still resting on the table, Madame spoke without her accent, "Chi-Chi, remember to pass on our message. Our families need to know we didn't do it on purpose. It was just our time to move on, and we like it better here. Please don't forget!"

Chimere fell back into the chair. Before she could stop herself, she cried out, "Why did you choose me? How am I supposed to know how to find all these families? I can't do it! Please, tell them to find someone else, please. I can't—" She put her hands over her face and sobbed. "I just want to sleep…please!"

"We don't trust anyone else, but we'll try. Rest now, Chi-Chi, rest now. You can trust your new friend's intentions. He really does respect your choices and cares more than he shows. God is going to use you more later. So rest now, Chi-Chi, rest now!" Abruptly, Madame Ulda stood and exited the room as oddly as she had entered.

They looked at one another, immobilized by what had just occurred. After a couple of minutes, Liby tapped Randella on the shoulder and whispered for her to get up. Chimere was already at the front door when they finally exited the room. No one spoke a word as they walked to the car. They rode the first ten minutes in silence.

Liby squirmed and then turned to Chimere. "So your nickname is Chi-Chi, like chichiwawa?" They all laughed as Liby leaned to turn on the radio. The whispery voice of Phil Collins "One More Night" encircled them. "But really, is Chi-Chi a nickname?" Liby asked sincerely.

"You know, it was college thing. I'd prefer not to be called that anymore."

Randella pulled into the parking lot next to Chimere's car. "Well, it was a pretty eventful night. Thanks for tagging along, Chimere. Your bein' there sure made it a lot more interesting, that's for sure."

"Yes, I suppose it did. So how much is my share?"

Liby offered to refill her cup for a final drink. Chimere declined and was opening her wallet to see how much cash she had on hand.

"Chimere, this one was on us. Like Rande said, you coming along made it really interesting. You think you'll want to go with us again?"

"No thanks, Liby. This one time was eventful enough for me." Chimere got out of the car. "I hope you ladies have a wonderful weekend. See you bright and early on Monday."

As she opened the car door, Randella rolled down her window. "See you Monday. Drive careful now."

Their waving hands were still visible as Randella drove off. Chimere got in her car and sat there, going over the words of Madame Ulda. She had asked for them to leave her alone, and it seemed they were going to honor that request. All she wanted was to have a good night's sleep without all the visits. *Anyway, why would any God want to use her and for what? What did she have to offer God?* She just wanted to help everyone in the struggle and fight for equality. Her mind was reeling as she drove home.

Kelly and Medan were in the living room talking when she walked in the door. Medan stood to his feet quickly, rushing to greet her. Kelly had a big smile of agreement on her face as she made her way to her room.

Medan instinctively just held her, not speaking a word. He felt a deep warmth when she wrapped her arms tightly around his midsection. He didn't care if they made it to the planned fundraising party. The comfort and joy he felt was all that mattered. When Chimere finally released her hold, Medan wasn't yet ready to feel that void. She looked up at him with tears in her eyes and a smile on her face. He took her sweet face in his hands, leaned over, and kissed her for the first time. His heart raced as she was more receptive than he had anticipated. He was glad he listened to Kelly, because she had finally warmed up to him. Her arms were now wrapped around his neck, and her hands rubbed the base of his neck, sending shivers and goose bumps all over. He pulled back, looked into her eyes, and smiled.

"Thanks, Medan! I'm so glad you were here." She rested her hands on his forearms and squeezed. "Oh, sorry I kept you waiting. I completely forgot we have the NAACP Christmas fundraiser. This was the best welcome home I could ask for though."

"I'm glad I was here for that myself! I would love to have this same welcoming for you every night. We can be fashionably late for a change. Take your time getting ready. I'll be right here waiting."

Chimere smiled up at him, then she ran her fingers through his goatee before she turned and walked away.

FLIGHT INTO THE LIGHT

Chimere emerged into the living room after about fifteen minutes. Medan couldn't take his eyes off her face. She was glowing with her hair pulled in a bun at the top of her head. She wore a burnt orange halter dress with gold high-heeled sandals and accessories.

Kelly came out of her room heading for the kitchen and stopped to gawk at her friend. "Whoa, Chimere! Girl, you're as bright as the sun. You looking good, girlfriend! I didn't think that color was you, but I swear, you have a spotlight on. Doesn't she look incredible, Medan?"

Medan walked over to stand next to Kelly. "Well, I have to be honest. You are right Keke, she is beaming! I'm glad she's going to be in my—I mean, on my arm tonight!" He took Chimere by the hands and twirled her around, which lifted the skirt of her dress showing her thighs. He whistled.

He and Kelly laughed as Chimere did a runway strut to the middle of the living room.

She giggled. "Thanks, you two. You've made me feel so much better now." She walked over to Medan and placed her arms around his neck as she tiptoed to kiss him on his nose. "Shall we go, my king? We've made them wait long enough. Time for the king and queen to make their entrance."

They all laughed as Medan opened the door. He kissed Kelly on the forehead and grabbed the golden shawl for his queen to wear later. They walked down the stairs hand in hand as Kelly watched like an approving parent until they were both in the truck.

It warmed her heart watching Medan kiss Chimere on the cheek after she was seated in the truck. This was going to just get better. She smiled as she realized her best friend and Jim's best friend were going to be a couple at their wedding. She closed the door, but stood there for a moment. She then skipped off to the kitchen and grabbed the phone to call Jim.

When Jim answered, all he heard was her indecipherable shrieking in his ear. He caught Medan and Chimere's names at the beginning of the squall and a kiss somewhere that led to the only conclusion. They finally had a moment. Medan had finally melted the ice.

She finally slowed down and lowered her voice to a less screechy pitch, making sure to point out how she always knew they would make a great couple. This was perfect: her maid of honor and Jim's best man will become a couple. She hoped Chimere would catch the bouquet or Medan to grab the garter.

Jim could only chuckle at the idea of his other best girl with his best friend. He knew Medan was hooked after the party. With the Theron incident, his concern was making sure Chimere got through the trial. He was happy that his friend finally found her. Maybe now he wouldn't have to listen to Medan talk about her every ten minutes.

Chimere was ecstatic when she won the silent auction—a weekend getaway to Savannah. *This would be a great honeymoon gift for Jim and Kelly*, she thought. Medan had won something, but he wouldn't tell her what it was. She enjoyed the attention she was getting from him. It made her want to stick her chest out at the way he doted on her.

He made efforts to keep her on the dance floor as much as he could. In heels, she was just the right height for him to rest his chin on the top of her head. He loved the way she fit right beneath his arms, right where she belonged—his missing rib.

The night was filled with moving conversations with many of the friends they met and connected with at some other mixer or fundraising event. The night concluded with them promising to meet up for the gift sorting at the church the next morning.

When they got to the truck, Chimere paused after Medan opened the truck door. "Would you be angry with me if I told you I wasn't ready to go home yet? I don't have any particular place in mind. I'm just not ready to call it a night."

"Well I'm fine with that, just as long I'm hanging out with you. Chimere, you have been playing that hard-to-get role for almost six months now, why are you so skittish? I'm not going to hurt you, I promise."

"It's not that I'm skittish, Da'Man! It's more like I don't want to waste anyone's time, especially not mine. I have a ten-year plan, and it's difficult to find someone who is willing to work with me. So it's best for me to do what I need to reach my goals and hope I meet the right man."

"What makes you think you haven't already met the right man? How do you know the right man doesn't have a ten-year plan too? Are you willing to compromise or are your goals carved in stone?" She put her arms around his neck and looked him straight in the eye. "I'm serious, Chi-Chi. Are you willing to compromise? Whose career would take a backseat?"

"Why would either career need to suffer? Why, do you think I'm so inflexible that I wouldn't be willing to be the good woman at the side of a good man?"

"Are you willing to be my good woman?"

"Well, Mr. Freeman, I—yes, I would be willing to be the good woman at your side. I'm not going to promise that I'll always be willing to compromise. I will do my best to be flexible."

"Well, I'd say we've got lots to talk about and some plans to make apparently, Miss Royle! Can I tell you something and promise me not to laugh?"

"Medan, one thing you are not is funny. So, sure, what is it?"

"I've known since I saw you at a Step Off a couple of years ago that one day, I was going to make you my wife."

"Wait, hold on a second! You are not asking me to marry you, are you?"

"No, not yet. You'll know when I do. I just know that you are the woman I want to spend the rest of my life with and raise a family with. I know there is no one else out there I want to learn and love until I'm old and gray."

"That's sweet, and I'm flattered. Can we just take it one step at a time? Our first step is making sure Jim and Kelly get married without any major catastrophe!"

"I think they have it well under control. All the groom's men are fitted for their tuxes. We all have appointments for haircuts and shaves. The room for the bachelor party is already paid for. Your girl is organized and very finicky. Jim has been a soldier marching to her drum and staying on the beat. He's made me think about not wasting anymore time. Life is too short to keep—"

"To keep playing the field?"

"No, to keep waiting and letting the woman I want to have my children keep pushing me away!"

"For your information, I never pushed you away. I just kept you at a distance. I knew I wanted to get to know you at the party. I was just kidding when I said I sat on your lap to see some other guy. You've been the only man I've been willing to give up some of my precious time for. I just wanted to achieve some of the goals I set. It was important for me to do this, so I can maintain the sense of accomplishment. You understand that, don't you? Honestly, I don't care if my career goals have to change in order to be with a good man. I'm especially glad you chose me. I wasn't afraid of your reputation because I knew—well, let's just say, I trusted the voice in my head. I'm sorry I made you work so hard."

"Well, baby, you are worth every ounce of sweat that crossed my brow. I just have one question, what happened to dude who was trying to block me? You know that Alpha, the one who was getting a lot of your time?"

"I've been waiting for you to ask me that. I had an answer all ready for you, but now it is simpler to just tell you. The morning after the party, he…uh—crap! He…um…was sentenced to fifteen years for aggravated assault. The judge was so insulted by his attitude he told him that even with good behavior, he wouldn't be eligible for parole until he served at least half the max." She took a deep breath and wiped her brow. "*Phew!* That was easier than I thought it was going to be. It's all over, thank God. He's where he can't hurt anyone else."

"Well, good. I'm just glad he's not jocking you. What was it about him, Chimere? Why was he always around, and you gave me a hard time?"

She hugged him and kissed him. "He was nothing special. I guess I was just comfortable with him because I wasn't into him. Let's get out of here!"

"At your service, Miss Royle! Lead on!"

He held the door open for her, then he jumped in the driver's seat of his truck, and off they drove toward Chimere's apartment. When they got there, she asked him to please stay with her until she fell asleep. Telling him about Theron had stirred some old feelings and flashbacks. Medan woke with a smile on his face when he realized he had slept with her in his arms the entire night. He chuckled when he looked at her hair, spread wildly all over her head and mascara slightly smeared around both eyes. It was the best sleep he'd had in a long time. It was the first time in years he'd slept in his clothes and not been intoxicated.

While attempting to sit up, he noticed out of the corner of his eye that Kelly was standing at the door with a big smile as she watched them. She waved at him and gently closed the door. He tried to free himself without waking Chimere up. She looked so peaceful and sweet. When he was just about to inch off the bed, Chimere rolled over, kissed him, and went back to sleep. He smoothed her hair down and pulled the blanket around her. He stood there, watching her sleep for a minute then left the room.

Kelly had set up two cups. "Good morning, Medan! Surprised to see you here. Would you like a cup of coffee? I'm going to make couple of eggs. Can I fix you some?"

"A cup of coffee is fine."

He stood at the kitchen bar as Kelly poured him a hot cup of coffee. He took a seat at the table. From the containers set up on the table, he added a little milk and sugar. Kelly came to join him. They sat drinking their coffee in silence. He caught Kelly smiling at him, and all he could do was shake his head.

"Go on, say it. I know it's bubbling up in your mouth right now." He reached over to tap the top of her hand. She caught his hand before he could tap her and clasped both her hands around his. "Kelly, I am so glad you were right. She fits! That's the best way to describe how it feels being with her."

"I knew you were the man for her all along. It was something in the air when you two were in close proximity to each other. I love it! It makes me happy to know Chi-Chi is happy. You seem to keep a smile on her face. Don't ever stop, or you will have to deal with me. You know about Theron, right?"

"She told me he was in jail for assault. I know there is more because of the look on her face. Don't tell me anything.

I need her to trust me to tell me herself. I hope she tells me soon, because my mind is going places—"

"Oh, believe me, you don't need worry. You slept in her bed. She is going to tell you."

Medan laughed before taking his last drink of coffee. "We slept in our clothes. Your I-told-you-so speech is one I don't mind hearing. I've always hated going to some of these fundraisers, but she makes them fun. Everything I do with this woman brings me joy. Kelly, I really need to thank you for being right. I love Chimere!"

"Well, it's nice to know how you feel about me. How about you tell me about it?" Chimere, now dressed in T-shirt and shorts, walked over and sat on his lap. He wrapped one arm around her waist and kissed her on the cheek. "Well, what's the problem? I come in the room and the conversation ends?"

"Well, that depends on how long you were standing there," Kelly blurted out as she sipped her coffee.

"I was standing there long enough to know this would be a good time to get the whole story off me once and for all." Chimere took his face in her hands and kissed him. "It's not a pretty story, but I'm ready to forgive and move on. Medan, please know it's over, and he got what he deserved."

"When you put it like that, it does make me curious. I don't have any plans. Saturday is a good day for storytelling. I'm in the mood for a story with a happy ending. That is the kind of story this is, right?"

Chimere held his face in her hands as she recounted the events. Then Kelly told him the rest of the story: about her being half-nude and beating Theron with a book. Medan had to put Chimere off his lap because he was laughing so hard.

"I don't understand why everyone has that reaction." Kelly giggled as she left the table to take her shower. She had plans. Jim was going to pick her up for the cake-tasting. She was trying to stop making him wait on her. She promised him their wedding would start on time.

He explained it so sweetly the night he proposed to her. He told her that four years of college was already taking up two percent of the ten-percent brain he used, and she filled the other eight percent. He waited like she asked until after graduation. He wanted her to be his wife and mother of his children.

Kelly chose the day after Valentine's so they would have a double celebration of their love for the rest of their lives. Her dress was a beautiful pearl white and baby pink for the bridal party. Jim would be wearing a pearl-white tux and the groomsmen were in light-gray with purple tie and cummerbund. All the details were working out down to the pearl-white runner and baby-pink roses for the flower girl to toss.

Alice and Kevin had already purchased their tickets. The months seemed to fly by as if in a race to the finish line. The more she planned, the faster the days went. She was glad she had Jim's mother and Chimere helping her not have a complete nervous breakdown. Although she wanted to be married in a church, she was all right when her future in-laws insisted the ceremony and reception be at their home in Dunwoody. She and Jim were planning to spend Christmas with Jim's family. Work kept Chimere so busy she was glad they were going to stay close to home for Christmas.

Medan had canceled his trip to California to visit his family, so he could stay and help with the wedding preparations. Spending this Christmas with Chimere was top of his list, so to cancel was not a disappointment for him. There would be plenty more family Christmases, but now with the addition of the love of his life.

Chimere's parents were on a European trip since Samara was attending Howard University. She loved that her parents were finally doing the things she heard them talk about growing up. She was even more excited to be with the man she knew was meant for her for the rest of her life. This would be their first Christmas together. She couldn't wait to give Medan the gift she found for him—a beautiful replica bust of Queen Nefertiti.

As a group, it was decided they were going to have a quiet Christmas Eve dinner, just the four of them at Medan's house. He went all out on the decorations but kept his fraternity color scheme of purple and gold. He had a friend cater the meal for them. He had all the old Motown Christmas albums set to play through the meal.

Medan greeted them at the door in a Santa hat and a silver tray containing crystal cups of spiked eggnog with a sprinkle of nutmeg on top. The fireplace was burning, and the rooms were filled with a toasty warmth. The eggnog and rum helped them warm up to go out to the backyard for the lighting of the manger Medan had set up for them. They had a wonderful meal and great conversation. Jim and Kelly were trying to get out before all the traffic hit, but Medan convinced them to stay just a little longer. They returned to the living room in front of the fireplace, sharing stories of family Christmases.

Jim noticed Medan looking at the clock repeatedly and sticking his hand in his pocket. Jim grinned at him. "Hey, Med, its midnight. Me and Kelly really need to head out. We have a big day tomorrow. We have to be at my parents' by ten, or my mother will be serving my head."

"It's midnight? Boy, time sure did fly. Okay, just one more drink!"

He rushed over to the bar and brought glasses of champagne. He handed Jim and Kelly a glass then he knelt down in front of Chimere. Kelly sighed as tears began to roll down her cheeks. Chimere was glowing and smiling brighter than she ever had.

"Chimere, never has a woman turned me into a stalker." They all laughed. "But from the first time I saw you, when you were a pledging. I knew you were not like any of these women here. I didn't approach you because I didn't want to scare you away. Back then, I knew I wasn't ready for anything serious. I never dreamed I would find someone to make me feel like I feel when I'm with you. I've loved you for so long, and to finally have you melt into my arms every day, I can't imagine spending the rest of my life not feeling this way every day. You have given me back my rib, and I know with you by my side, I can do anything. I will do everything in my power to make sure you keep this smile on your face. Chimere Royle, will you accept this ring along with my love and spend the rest of your life with me?"

With tears in her eyes, Chimere nodded yes. He opened the jewelry box that had been burning a hole in his pocket. Chimere and Kelly gasped at the same time when the light hit the emerald-cut pink diamond in a gold setting. He placed the ring on her finger, she jumped on him, sending them crashing to the floor. They all laughed. Medan looked at her and laughed even harder.

"Well, I can honestly say you knock me off my feet, Chimere!"

The laughter was ringing as the sounds of Johnny Mathis serenaded them with "Winter Wonderland". After getting off the floor, they all began singing along with Johnny in between spurts of laughter. They hugged one another and said good-night. They stood in the doorway waving until Jim and Kelly were out of sight. Just as they closed the front door, Medan's phone rang.

"Merry Christmas, Momma!"

"How did you know it was me, son?" She laughed. This was their family Christmas ritual since her four children were in different parts of the country. If they didn't make it for any large holiday, the midnight phone call was made.

"Momma! No one that matters would be calling me this time of night. Where is Pops?"

"You know your father is in bed. I had to call and wish you a Merry Christmas. So…did you ask your young lady? Did she say yes?"

"Momma, she's right here. So how about I let you speak to her yourself, and you ask her."

He tried to hand Chimere the phone, but she kept pushing it away. He finally just put the receiver to her ear. He could hear his mother asking question after question. He laughed as Chimere would start to answer just as his mother shot off another question. Chimere was slapping him on his arm, while he kept his hand over his mouth to muffle his laughter. Chimere finally ended the conversation, promising to visit soon. Medan hung up the phone, grabbed her, and just held her tightly in his arms. He kissed her on top of her head and began singing "Special Lady" while he danced her around the living room. When he finished the song, he stopped in front of the Christmas tree. Then he picked up a small box and placed it in her hands.

"Go on, open it! It's after midnight, so it's early Christmas morning. It's just something simple."

Chimere ripped the paper off the box. She opened the lid to find a sheet of paper folded in half. She opened the paper, laughed at the drawing, and read the note. "The holder of this coupon is entitled to a lifetime of faithfulness, love, security, companionship, gratitude, friendship, loyalty, and dedication to supporting your dreams. All my heart Medan4ever, Ya Man!" Underneath the note was gold sideways heart with a cross cutting through the heart. Chimere wept.

Medan moved closer, wiped her tears, and kissed her. "Baby, what? You don't like it?"

"No, Medan, I love it and I love you. This is the most thoughtful gift I've ever received. Don't you ever forget, I got this in writing, so you better not mess up, ever."

"*Phew!* I thought I already messed up. Come on, let me get you home."

"Medan, I actually brought my clothes for tomorrow. I just figured it would easier to leave from here. You're closer to the 285. It's all right if I stay the night, right?"

"Chimere, you know you can stay here. Let me make up the guest room for you."

"Um…I was thinking—only if it wouldn't be a problem…I was thinking it would be nicer to sleep in your arms."

"Oh, heck yeah! Girl, you know I love holding you whether you're awake or asleep."

He took her by the hand and led her to his room. He left the room to allow her privacy to change. She put on her babydoll pajamas and crawled into the bed. She called to him after she was settled. He came back wearing pajama pants and a T-shirt. He turned off the lights and crawled in bed. She curled herself close to him, and he wrapped her in his arms. This was the best Christmas present she could give him. Having her in his arms was all he could have asked for. It didn't matter his arm was numb or his mouth full of her hair.

The ringing of the phone woke them. Medan didn't want to break from the embrace he had her in. He looked at her expression. He nudged her and whispered for her to answer since she was the closest. She answered and had to pull the receiver from her ear. The volume of the voices on the other end was at a decibel she was not accustomed to. Medan was laughing so hard he fell off the bed. His mother was screaming into the phone.

"Oh, dear Lord! Is this my future daughter-in-law?"

"Yes, Mrs. Freeman. Merry Christmas!"

"Well, my dear Chimere. You can call me Mom or Felicity. I look forward to meeting you. I don't know what you did to him, but I've never heard my son speak so highly of any woman. We have lots to talk about and, thankfully, we have a lifetime to do that. Oh my! I almost forgot. We will meet in February at Jim and Kelly's wedding. Jim has been our other son since Medan took him under his wing. He is a wonderful young man. He came to our rescue on many occasions when Medan was running the frat they are a part of. I met Kelly once, and she seems like a lovely girl. They are very well-suited."

Chimere was trying to hand Medan the phone, but he kept pushing it away. "Thank you, Mrs. Free—I mean, Felicity. I look forward to meeting you all at the wedding. Well, here is your son. Nice speaking with you."

She dropped the phone on the bed, jumped up, and grabbed her bag as she ran off to the bathroom. She didn't want to eavesdrop, so she turned on the shower. She pulled her clothes from her bag. The steam would be good before a long day of festivities. She stared in the mirror blindly, her mind drifted off to how happy she was. She was grateful the dreams had stopped once she allowed herself to admit Medan took her breath away. She played with the ring for a moment, brushed her teeth, and then jumped in the shower. She plugged in her curling iron and wiped the steam from the mirror. She opened the door a crack to help clear the steam. The mirror was clear, and her curling iron was the perfect temp by the time she was dressed. Medan was freshly shaven, standing outside the bathroom when she opened the door.

"Baby, I wanted to tell you before I forget. I had a dream of a young boy with bluish lips. He was in a white robe. He called himself 'Ready Eddie' and told me I better keep you protected always. It was strange because he spoke about you like he knew you. Then he said if I slacked off, he would be back." He shrugged his shoulders. "I never remember my dreams, but this one…it felt like I was speaking with him just like we're doing now."

Chimere smiled as she reached up and rubbed his head. "Oh my goodness! That is a very interesting dream. If I were you, I wouldn't mess around. You best be listening if you don't want 'Ready Eddie' to come back." She laughed, but she didn't know what to think or what to do. *Should she tell him she knew Eddie? No way! He would think she was cuckoo!* "No slacking, Mr. Freeman!"

He grabbed her and kissed her. "Well, if Eddie knew what I knew, he would have known he didn't need to tell me not to slack. My greatest desire is to keep this beautiful face smiling! I love you so much, Chimere, and I promise to never slack on that, not ever. I was thinking…how would you feel about an August wedding in California?" He went to the tree to start bagging up the gifts. He sat on the sofa and patted the cushion next to him. "I know that's a long way for a lot of people to travel, but my mother wants me to get married in our family church."

Chimere came and sat on his lap. "Baby, I would marry you in Timbuktu. I don't care about any of the hoopla. All I want is to spend the rest of my life being loved and loving you, Medan!" She looked at her watch, jumped off his lap, and slapped him on his thigh. "Come on, big guy. It's already almost one o'clock, we have a Christmas party to get to." She grabbed her purse along with one of the bags of gifts and had her hand on the knob.

He placed his hand over hers to stop her from opening the door. He looked at her for a moment, bent down and kissed her puckered lips. "Now if you are going to marry me, then you better stop trying to do my job. My momma didn't raise no slouch. I know my role in this relationship. I am Da'Man, and don't you forget it!"

He opened the door, took her by the hand, and led her out the door. He grabbed the other bag of gifts and closed the door. After she got settled in truck, he placed the bag of gifts on her lap. "Good girl! I'll have you trained by the time you walk down the aisle." He laughed as he closed the door before she could respond.

When he got around to the driver's door, she had locked him out. He was laughing, because she was still pouting. He opened the door and jumped in. He turned to her and ran his hand to smooth her hair.

She grabbed his hand, kissing each fingertip. "You don't have to do any training. My mom did a very good job. You just need to make sure you stay on your Ps and Qs, and we'll be just fine." She pulled down the visor to check her lips.

He laughed as he closed the door. He leaned over and kissed her on the cheek before he started the engine and sped off toward the highway. As they entered the almost empty freeway, he slipped his fingers in between her fingers and rested them on her knee. He was relieved the drive was uncomplicated by non-driving holiday people.

They arrived just as Jim and Kelly were unpacking the trunk. Medan pulled up next to Jim. Medan jumped out and simultaneously they greeted each other as frats then hugged as brothers. Medan walked back to the truck, grabbed the bags, and opened the door for Chimere. Chimere rushed over to Kelly so quickly they almost fell over. They laughed as they walked up the front stairs to the beautiful, very southern-style Smalls' home.

Chimere was in awe at the enormity of the house. She felt like she had stepped back in time. The antebellum architecture made the house more fascinating, and the allure of old south caught her. She loved the large columns and the shutters on the upper floor windows. The porch encircled the entire house, and the trees and flowers made her feel lost in time.

"Whoa, Jim! I didn't realize…um…this house is amazing! This is the perfect place for the wedding. I can't even imagine you in this house. I was expected a much smaller house from the way you spoke about home. So do y'all have servants?"

Jim stopped at the top step and looked at Chimere. "I didn't realize until just now this is the first time you've been here. I know I made it seem like I grew up living in a shack. But you know what would happen if I told people my father is a retired pro-football player and my mom is a chef with three restaurants." He opened the front door and moved to the side to let them all enter. "That's why I was very selective about who I got close to. I thought you knew, Chi-Chi. Sorry."

"It's cool. I understand, because I'm the same way. You know if you tell some folks you have a little family money, they will have their hand out every time you see them. But Jim, this is more than a little money. This house is—is—*gee-whiz*! I don't even have words other than it's beautiful." They all laughed. Chimere gasped when she stepped inside the entry.

The entry was very well-lit by the large dome skylight that covered almost the entire ceiling. There were golden staircases on each side of the entryway. The entry for the two large rooms on either side were bordered with real evergreen garlands intertwined with gold-and-white ribbons, divided by gold bells hung in the center from gold wires. Softly playing in the background were Christmas carols throughout the entire first floor.

Beneath the staircase was the fullest Christmas tree she had ever seen. It was decorated with gold ornaments and topped with a lit golden angel surrounded by beautifully wrapped gifts of all shapes and sizes. Tables with white gold-trimmed tablecloths on either side of the tree were full with flowering poinsettias in the center, surrounded with six various-sized glass canisters, each filled with colorful candy and a scoop. Two smaller tables, covered with a gold cloth, were placed in front of the pillars containing red boxes of multiple sizes.

The living room to the left was full of large oversized furniture in warm cream and beige. In the front bay window, a seat was filled with more elegantly wrapped gifts. A smaller Christmas tree was decorated with what seemed to be all handmade ornaments and topped with a star. The fireplace was lined with eight, full, large stockings, a string of white lights, and Christmas cards all across the mantle. Above the mantle was a large portrait of the Smalls dressed in white.

The library to the right with its massive shelves full of books was strung with lights and garland. In the center of the floor was a replica of the house, enclosed by a track with a steaming train of eight cars slowly circling around it. Each car had the name of a family member that held a wrapped gift and a caboose filled with gold-wrapped candy packs. In one of the large armchairs was a stuffed Santa saying, "Ho, Ho, Ho! Merry Christmas!" and two elves on each side, holding large candy canes.

The landing of the second floor held the most extravagant nativity under the large arch. The figurines were so lifelike, even the animals looked real. Hung from the ceiling, just above the manger, was an angel in flowing white robes holding a golden harp. The baby Jesus was in a backlit cradle, surrounded by Mary, Joseph, four shepherds holding gifts, four sheep, two cows, and a goat.

When they reached the second floor, Medan asked Jim, "Tell me again, why are there shepherds and not the three wise men?"

"Aw, man! Seriously? You have heard this story at least forty times." He looked over at Medan, who was casually nodding his head toward Chimere. "Oh, all right! There are only shepherds because Luke 2:15–16 says, 'And it came to pass, as the angels were gone away from them into heaven, the shepherds said one to another, Let us now go even unto Bethlehem, and see this thing which is come to pass, which the Lord hath made known unto us. And they came with haste, and found Mary, and Joseph, and the babe lying in a manger.' So the truth is, the shepherds were there within the first forty days of his birth. The wise men didn't come around until Jesus was a little older. If we were to include the wise men, my mother would never allow for it to be three. That is a whole other sermon. Come on, let me show you the rest of the house. My mom has kept all our rooms like they were before we moved out. So no laughing or snide comments allowed."

After viewing the upstairs, they headed down to the living room. Mrs. Smalls was waiting for them at the entrance with a tray of glass mugs filled with hot spiced apple cider. Introductions were made as they walked from the living room into the large dining room. Two tables had been set up with angel wings place cards for each guest. The tables were set so his parents; Uncle Darin, his father's younger brother and Aunt Andriana; Aunt Lizzy, his mother's older sister, and Uncle John; two older brothers, Jeff Jr. and Joshua; their wives Ginger and Leslie; Jim and Kelly; and Medan and Chimere were seated at one table. The other table was filled by Jim's younger sister, Jazmine and younger brother, Jeremiah, three nieces, and three nephews.

The main discussion was of the pending plans and date for Jim and Kelly's wedding. The meal served was a traditional southern menu of turkey and stuffing, collard greens with okra, chitterlings, macaroni and cheese, candied yams, mashed potatoes, gravy, honey butter cornbread, and jellied cranberry sauce. The buffet at the rear of the room held the desserts. There was apple pecan pie, sweet potato pie, peach cobbler, chocolate cream, lemon cake, and red velvet cake. The butler made his final appearance after bringing out several bottles of wine and punch bowl of raspberry frappe. The muffled clanging of the pots could be heard off in the distance as the family talked and laughed.

After about an hour, most everyone was sitting back in their seats, too full to move. The conversation turned to congratulations for Jazmine's acceptance to Grambling State to obtain a BA in Business. Jazmine's impassioned speech against fraternities and sororities got the conversation heated. She finally resolved not to discuss this topic with her family ever again after she realized that everyone at the other table was part of one. After the meal, they were directed to the family room. Of all the rooms Chimere had seen, this one was her favorite. Flowers and plants filled each of the three bay windows. There was a small fireplace with more Christmas cards along the mantle. An extra-large, multi-paned, double-glass door led to a spectacular flower garden.

Should the weather permit, this was going to be the setting for the wedding. The room had two large puffy pink sofas and four floral chairs. A pink-leather chaise lounge was near a small shiny white piano. On one wall was a built-in entertainment center with rolling doors. There was a stereo complete with a reel-to-reel and turntable. The shelves below held at least three hundred albums, two hundred or so cassette tapes, and a great collection of old and current VCR movie tapes.

Jim took a seat at the piano and began to play. Everyone started to fan throughout the room as Kelly began singing "O Holy Night." The sound of the applause echoed in the room. Kelly sang a few more Christmas songs. She gracefully encouraged the family to join her in "Silent Night."

Once in the living room conversations of Christmas' past were recalled with laughter and some sorrowful hearts. They were all grateful for the unity they had and how blessed they were to be together for another holiday. The younger children raced to see who would get the closest spot on the floor near the tree, bumping each other without knocking over the tree. Wearing a Santa hat, Jeff "Jazz" Smalls entered rolling a cart full of hot chocolate, coffee, and eggnog. He then went to sit on an ottoman near the tree. He began with the youngest and worked his way to his wife. Then the rest of the family exchanged gifts before Jazz called for prayer, which was the traditional signal the celebration had come to an end. They gathered in a circle in the entryway with packages at their feet.

Jazz began. "All eyes closed, heads bowed, and minds clear. Lord, we come before you with grateful hearts. We thank you for this expansion of our family. We ask you to continue to forgive us as you direct our steps and as we venture among your people. Cover us with your mercy as we travel these holiday roads. We ask you to keep our hearts and minds in perfect peace as we give honor and thanks to you for the birth of your son, Jesus. Thank you, Lord. Amen!"

Chimere couldn't believe they had been there for a little over five hours. She didn't want to say good-bye to anyone. She adored this family and was glad Kelly was already a very big part of it. It didn't even bother her too much about being in a prayer circle. She realized it had been a few days since she'd had a chance to really speak with Kelly. Seeing the glow of joy surrounding her friend made her smile. *What a way to end a year!*

Path to Glory

Saturday, February 15, 1986, was a very cool day in Atlanta. No sign of snow or rain, so things were still on course. After breakfast, the entire bridal party, along with the mothers of the bride and groom, gathered in the entryway for prayer led by Alice, Kelly's mom. Her words touched everyone, bringing watery eyes and genuine smiles of joy. It was like a football huddle with *Amen* being the signal to break and go.

Occasional collisions with the decorating staff were occurring as the women rushed about the Smalls' home. Chimere got lost a couple of times, trying to find the less traveled route to the bride's room. Her desire was to ensure a perfect day for Kelly. Getting all the women's hair and makeup done and dressed finished without messing up either one was exhausting, but Chimere handled it with complete calm and a constant smile.

The entryway was now filled with pink-and-white roses in beautiful vases atop golden pillars. Where the Christmas tree had been was now blocked off by satin pink drape with a photo collage of the bride and groom, filling most of it. To the left, surrounded with pink roses, was a pedestal that held the pink gilt-edged guest book and two gold pens. To the left was a white satin-covered table on which the wedding favors had been placed.

The living and dining rooms were transformed into a rose garden with more pillars of pink-and-white roses. Each room had ten tables set for ten with pink table clothes, gold-rimmed white china, and gold place settings. The center pieces were oblong gold-lipped crystal trays half-filled with pink pearls and gold beads intertwined with seven pink crisscrossed calla lilies. Set atop the plates were small engraved golden treasure chests with the name of each guest on top, the date on back, and the names of bride and groom at the front.

The family room had been transformed into a ball room with large candle-filled crystal chandeliers. The sweet sound of the band invigorated the women as they made the finishing touches. The fireplace was burning extra hot to take the chill off from the doors being open. A pink satin runner was in place at the door with pedestals of white roses on either side, spanning the small porch and down five stairs. Leading down an aisle, separating ten rows of ten chairs on each side on every other row were golden poles with a trio of iridescent glass hearts. The pink runner ended at the now floral-covered, garden-trellis structure. Under the trellis was a small pedestal for the minister and a table covered with a pink satin cloth, and white rose petals were sprinkled around the large cylindrical white unity candle.

Chimere was making her last check of the seating arrangement when the band completed its warm-up and soundcheck. She strolled into the room to a rendition of Junior Walker's "What Does It Take." She couldn't resist doing a few twirls to the bluesy rhythm of the horns. Her last twirl landed her right in Medan's arms.

"Hey! Oh no! The men are here? I better get back upstairs. I love you, man! See you in a little while." Smiling up at him, not budging from his embrace.

"Chi, is this how you want our wedding?"

"Oh, honey, not at all. This is more than I could even dream of. It is beautiful, and Kelly deserves this. I'm so happy for her." Still relaxed in his embrace, she stopped to brush away a tear. "Not that my dad wouldn't move heaven and earth to give me this, but this isn't me. I've never really put much thought into a wedding. Well, that is, not until you asked me to marry you and mentioned California. How would you feel about a small beach wedding?"

"You better get upstairs. We can discuss this later. I will remind you, though. My mother has her heart set on all of her children being married in a church." He turned her in the direction of the stairs and kissed her on her shoulder. "Now get! By the way, you take my breath away, and I'm digging you in that dress!"

Chimere blew him a kiss before lifting her skirt to dash up the stairs. She was slightly out of breath when she reached the bride's room.

Alice pulled the door open. "Oh, thank God! There you are, Chimere! Kelly was having a tantrum because you weren't here. I see the men have arrived, so we need to pick up the pace a little bit. How are things downstairs?"

Chimere entered the room and went to the table for a glass of water. "It is amazing down there! I did final check, everything is perfect. Mrs. Smalls, this is all just so wonderful. Mama Alice, calm down! I think you are more nervous than Kelly. Let me go take care of our bride. In twenty minutes, I need Mrs. Smalls and Mama Alice to go downstairs to greet the guest. Bridesmaids, your bouquets are on a table at the entrance to the family room."

She walked over to stand behind Kelly, looking at her reflection in the boutique-style floor-length mirror. She pushed aside the veil and lightly kissed Kelly on the cheek. "You look like a princess! Everything is perfect, and in a few minutes, you are going to be Mrs. Kelly Smalls. I am so happy for you! Let's make this happen, baby!"

The bridesmaids were in pink-silk fitted mermaid dresses with fancy cut lace for the neckline and sleeve. All wore pearl necklaces and teardrop pearl earrings. They got in procession order and headed to the garden. Each bouquet was comprised of three medium-stemmed white rose tied together with gold ribbon. The band was playing the intro of Anita Baker's "Sweet Love," which was their cue to make their way to the family room entrance. A hush came over the group as the first bridesmaid came to the entrance. Each of the six made their way down the stairs to their waiting groomsman and whispered voices of approval.

After Medan and Chimere made their way down the aisle, the start of the traditional wedding march boomed through the speakers. Everyone rose to their feet as Kelly and her brother, Kevin stood in the entrance. Her face was barely visible through the glittery veil. The setting sun hitting the crystal-studded bodice of her dress made her glow as Kevin took her hand and led her down the porch stairs. The train of the dress covered the entire staircase as they made their way into the covered sitting area.

The Ohs and Ahs were coming from both sides of the guests. Kevin, grinning proudly with damp eyes, tightly hugged and kissed his little sister before handing her off to Jim, whose smile was wide as a slice of cake. Jim beamed even more as he took Kelly's hand. The hush came over the crowd again as the Minister began with the traditional "Dearly beloved."

Chimere tried to hold back the tears of joy, but with each I do, she allowed another tear to drop. She glanced over at Medan, and seeing his smile gave her comfort. Then she noticed the other bridesmaids were tearing up too. She looked out over the guest and saw more hankies and tissue being passed around. Yelps of pleasure when the matrimonial kiss took place were thunderous. The joy was so overwhelming as the Minister presented the new couple to the guest as "Mr. and Mrs. James Smalls."

A vocalist had joined the band when they began to play. The guests made their way to the room that was setup for the meal. Some couples danced to "I'll Be Good to You" by Rene and Angela. After the doors to the garden were closed, the band switched back to all soft jazz instrumentals.

Once all the guests were seated and the appetizers were served, Medan stood up, tapping his spoon against his gold-fluted champagne glass.

"Good evening, everyone! I'd like to propose a toast, but first, I have to say something to Jim. Man, when I met you seven years ago, you were just this wide-eyed, clumsy, and lanky silly boy. Today, I'm proud to call you best friend and brother for life. To Kelly, girl, you must be strong and courageous to hook up with this dude. Thank you for taking him off my hands." Everyone laughed. "No, but seriously, I see so much love and joy when I watch you two. Man, I was jealous of you for having found one of the good ones. You two are so well-suited for each other. I'm grateful to be here sharing this wonderful day with you both. I admire the faith you have in each other and God. I only hope when I get there, I have the same. I already know Jim can make good decisions. You chose me for your best man." He chuckled as he held up his glass. "To Mr. and Mrs. Smalls, may today be the beginning of many years of love, laughter, and prosperity. I love you both and look forward to many more years of us hanging out. Jumbo, Keke, best of everything to you both."

The clinking of glasses echoed through the room, and shouts of cheers rang out. The room was filled with laughter at the many different back-in-the-day tales of both the bride and the groom. After the meal was done, the guest slowly moved into the family room. Couples and singles took the dance floor as the band played "Slip N Slide" by Roy Ayers. As the band was packing up, the DJ began to play more dance music. He started it off with Prince's "Raspberry Beret," which set the tempo for the rest of the evening. The entrance of the bride and groom was announced by the DJ, followed by the intro to Forge M.D.'s "Tender Love" as they made their way to center of the floor. Slowly, other couples began to take the floor. The party began as the DJ changed gears with "Neutron Dance" by the Pointer Sisters. Kelly got the guest all revved up when she did her AKA call, and the dance floor went crazy with frat and sorority calls.

Finally, the newlyweds were ready to get to the airport for their honeymoon. Medan brought the gold Rolls Royce to the front door. The guest gathered outside as Kelly and Jim came rushing out. Kelly stopped to throw the bouquet and Jim threw the garter. One of their sorority sisters caught the bouquet, and Kevin, her brother, caught the garter. The couple drove off with the clinking of cans and a sign attached to the bumper that read, "Linked for Life."

When the last of the guest finally departed, it was after one in the morning. Chimere and Medan helped gather the gifts to take to the apartment she and Kelly shared. After they arrived and placed all the gifts in the living room, Chimere plopped into the oversized chair and wept. Medan came over, picked her up, sat her on his lap, and held her until she cried herself to sleep. He gently carried her to her bed. He watched her sleep for a moment then kissed her on the cheek. She woke up, grabbed his hand, and pulled him into the bed with her.

As she drifted off to sleep, he whispered, "Baby, you're not alone. I'm here and always will be."

Chimere was so excited when Kelly and Jim returned. It was now her turn to plan her dream wedding. The only downside was it meant she was going to be moving away from her best friend. During many of the evenings they had going through planning, she and Kelly would end up in tears. After which, Kelly would sing "Ain't No Mountain High Enough." Both were determined to keep the pact they made in second grade. They both knew this bond was greater than even sisters. The first time they thought they would be separated was when they were getting their college acceptance letters. Being accepted to Spelman on the same day brought much rejoicing in both homes. Now, they are both rejoicing at successfully reaching another goal. Chimere hoped the next four months to go by slowly.

The most difficult thing was trying to convince Felicity that the beach would be a wonderful location. Finally, Felicity agreed to find the perfect location. Within a few weeks, a location had been secured for her to have the perfect setting for their wedding day. Although she only saw photographs, Chimere was in agreement with the location near Shell Beach, California, with the reception to be held at the historical Madonna Inn. Once all details were worked out, the invitations were sent. Working with her future mother-in-law brought them closer than either thought was possible. They shared so much in common in many areas. Felicity was excited more and more after each conversation. It pleased her that her baby boy had found such a well-rounded young woman.

Chimere looked forward to their telephone conversations, because she found out so much about Medan. *Mother's always tell the best stories. I hope mine never tells Medan about some of my silliness.* She found out Medan was the youngest of three and the only son. He had been a spoiled brat and a momma's boy, but he always excelled in school. He had won many trophies for football. The family's biggest surprise was when he declined the scholarships from University of

Southern California and UCLA, deciding instead to move to Georgia to attend Morehouse. She learned that Medan had been a little bit of an activist. This was the driving force in choosing a historically Black college over two of the best universities in California.

Felicity had a PhD in business, started, and ran a small nonprofit, Heart of a Mother, which was geared toward assisting unwed mothers. She owned four houses that were open to young single mothers to live in. The clients were offered an alternative to putting their children up for adoption by giving them a place to live until they were gainfully employed. The young women were taught good housekeeping skills, how to save, how to budget, and how to prepare a healthy meal. In order to qualify for housing assistance, the women were required to attend fifteen counseling sessions. Chimere was enthralled with all the programs and jumped at Felicity's offer of a job after their move to California. Medan was offered a position at a power plant in California's Central Coast. Being the loving mother that she is, Felicity agreed to secure them a small rental near his job, setting a date for them to fly to California to begin a new life together.

TIME KEEPS ON SLIPPING

Sparta, Georgia, was only 102 miles east of Atlanta, but for Theron, it felt more like ten thousand. He was in disbelief that his sentence was so lengthy for just tossing around Chimere. He didn't mean to hurt her, and she wasn't that hurt. At least, when they finally went to trial, she looked fine. He only recalled striking her a couple of times and hadn't hit her that hard. He had a difficult time believing the damage he saw in the photographs was caused by him. He was certain, and he expressed it to his attorney, that somehow they had fixed those photos.

The medical reports had to be wrong. He loved Chimere. He would never hurt her like they were saying. The entire trial felt as if he were living someone else's life. It was difficult to watch his mother crying. It horrified him to see the looks on the faces of his brothers and sisters when the prosecuting attorney detailed the events of the beating and showed the photos.

It angered him Kelly wasn't brought up on charges for the injuries he sustained in her claimed defense of Chimere. The scar from his left brow to his right cheek would be a lifetime reminder of that morning. It seemed illogical this incident caused him to lose the love of his life. How could Chimere not feel the same way about him after all the time and affection he showered on her the last two years? What was wrong with her? He loved her, and for her to spurn him after all he'd been for her was more than he could accept. Then for her to defend that brute Medan was what caused him to snap that morning.

Theron knew he wasn't supposed to have any contact with Chimere, but he had to get her to see from his prospective. He had to make her understand how much he loved her. He wrote letter after letter, expressing how sorry he was for that morning. All he wanted was for her to forgive him and for them to return to their friendship. Every other day, he was immensely disappointed when the carefully written and decorative letters would be returned with big bold red letters that read, "Return to Sender." Each unopened letter was like a slap in the face, but he just didn't know how to let go. *How do you let go of the love of your life? How are you supposed to accept the one you love doesn't love you back?* He was really having a hard time understanding how Chimere couldn't see the future he had to offer her.

The group therapy sessions left him feeling even more unfulfilled, because no one saw things from his prospective. Some even said he needed to be a man about the whole thing and let it go. There were more women out there, and this one woman couldn't be the only one for him. He worked hard at being a model inmate. He learned early to keep his viewpoints and thoughts to himself. He developed relationships with the guards, which allowed him to obtain more freedom than others serving similar sentences. He worked his way to kitchen detail, where he realized his culinary gift. Soon, even the guards agreed he needed to be a cook full-time. The savory meals he prepared had everyone almost salivating by meal time.

The quest for appealing the length of his sentence was becoming futile, and eventually, he just stopped fighting. His family had even stopped coming to visit. The only consistent visitor he had was another friend, Lolita. Although her visits were regular, it left him plenty of time to work out how he would be able to win Chimere back when he was released. The prison psychiatrist had deemed him no longer a threat to himself or others. The warden had promised to write him a letter of recommendation because of his hard work.

Because he had actually finished his degree, the warden had placed him in a work program. He was the only inmate on a different schedule, because he worked closely with the warden in keeping records. Every year, the warden would push his case to the front of the list for parole hearings. All of which ended sadly for Theron. After each disappointing hearing, he would be allowed an extra hour or two in the kitchen to bake. It was a win-win for everyone. The staff and certain cell blocks would have a great dessert served with that evening's dinner.

He could still recall the first time the convicted Atlanta child murder, Wayne Williams was a part of the group sessions. The more time he spent with Wayne, the more he was beginning to believe in his innocence. He could see the sadness veiling his eyes while serving up his plate at mealtimes. Theron would try to make sure he would have a little something extra on his plate for dinner. Usually, he would put his vegetables in the shape of a smiley face, hoping to get him to smile. After five thousand, eight hundred and forty days of planning, the day of his release finally arrived.

The day he was released was both joyous and sad. He had established many bonds with many of the correctional officers and a few of the other inmates. He had learned more about the criminal mind than he ever imagined he would. The extensive therapy sessions had exposed him to some of the evilest minds Georgia housed within the walls of Hancock State Prison. When he walked outside the fence, which held him restrained, he was overjoyed Lolita was there waiting for him with open arms. Lolita had proven to be tried and true from the first time she came to visit. Anything he needed handled on the outside, he was able to rely on her eagerness to please him. He began to look forward to the uplifting loving letters from Lolita. She had become a great ally and friend over the last sixteen years.

Lolita had been ecstatic to comply when asked to keep an eye on Chimere. It made her feel like a Bond girl on an important case. When she told Theron about Kelly and Jim being married, she was surprised by his reaction. She never expected him to weep about such a wonderful event. Following Chimere, Kelly, and Jim every day for six months produced a thorough list of places frequented. She kept detailed journal entries of all the visitors. She kept a side journal, recording all visits from Medan. Her notes—with some assumptions—detailed what the two did once they were inside one another's homes. She was sad for Theron when she had to tell him Chimere had moved away with Medan.

She decided to wait telling him about their getting married, knowing it would anger him if she chose to wait until he was released to find out. The day the moving van pulled up, she found the announcement for their wedding in the pile of trash left at the curb. At least, she would be able to share the date they were to be married. Not only had Chimere and Medan moved, but so had Kelly and James. Lolita had been able to ascertain from a coworker of Kelly's that they had moved to possibly Arizona or Texas because of James' company relocating. She tried to befriend a couple of the women—whom she had seen Chimere with at the King Center—to see if she could get more information on where Chimere and Medan had moved. Since she had no information, she thought it would be best not to tell Theron anything until she did.

When he walked through the gate Lolita, hoped this was going to be the start of a whirlwind romance. She would be able to have the love of her life. Her hope was to be able to bring Theron back to life, back to feeling like he belonged. So much had changed since he had gone to jail. So many new things she would be able to teach him, hoping each lesson would make her more indispensable to him.

Theron was indebted to the Warden for getting him access to the computers and the on-line classes to help him stay up with where technology had progressed, making his bacherlor's degree in Computer Science still relevant and him more employable. He took the classes, learned, and developed more skills than even the warden was aware of. The more he learned, the more he wanted to be on the outside to have access to more knowledge and systems to hack. He had already set up a savings account with money he'd moved from some offshore accounts. To insure nothing could be traced back to him, he created a worm virus that would cause the end line go back to the bank from where the money was moved.

When the day arrived for Theron to be released, he'd given Lolita access to the accounts, so they would have enough to find a nice place to live. Saying good-bye to all the people took him a longer than he thought, but it was a happy farewell. He was finally going to be free to seek out the one woman he loved. The plans were firmly in his mind, and now, he would finally be able to put them into action. He had siphoned enough money for them to live comfortably for at least five years before either had to find some sort of employment.

Lolita had found a nice two-bedroom house in Dunwoody and furnished it modestly. She filled the closet with updated wardrobe for him, hoping he would acclimate to current fashion without too much of a challenge. She knew adjusting to life outside would take some time, especially with all the new advances of the last decade. Technology was advancing by leaps and bounds, even she was having a little difficulty keeping up. Advances Theron could not have possibly been exposed to behind prison walls.

Hoping to secure his love, she took months altering her appearance to mirror Chimere, but just enough difference to allow him to see her and forget all about his college crush. She needed him to want and desire her the way she wanted and desired him. She wanted to earn his heart, mind, body, and hopefully, a marriage proposal. Although she had a job at a little boutique in East Atlanta, the income she made wasn't enough. When he gave her the accounts and told her what to do with the money, she asked no questions. She didn't care how he had acquired all this money but was glad, because now she would really be able to show him how much she was in his corner.

As she stood outside Hancock Prison waiting for the love of her life, her hands began to sweat, and the humidity of the August morning was making her hair frizzy. Nervously, she tried to smooth the strands trying to stand out. She glanced in the side-view mirror checking her lipstick just as the gate open, and out walked Theron. He was dressed in the suit he had worn the last day of his trial. In her eyes, he looked amazing, and the fit of the suit was tighter because he had been working out. She couldn't wait to be wrapped in his now bulging arms.

As he reached the car, he turned and took a long anguished look at the place he called home for the last sixteen years. He smiled and jumped into the car without a word to Lolita. She looked at him, back at the prison, then got in, and started the engine. Her hopes of being with the man she loved were all that mattered. She would do whatever was necessary to keep this man in her life, willing to pay any price to be in his arms after all the years of waiting.

8

You Belong to Me

Theron had been waiting for the moment when he would be able to get Chimere alone. Finally, after a ten-year search all the planning and expenses had proven effective. He was just a few houses away, watching the comings and goings of the Freeman family. He would sit for days and only leave for brief moments to go clean up and eat once he had their schedule.

He knew Medan would leave the house at 6:15 every morning. Chimere would round up the kids, and usually, they would be out of the house by 7:30 or 7:45 at the latest. She and Kelly would meet for breakfast at Coco's in Pismo, which was midway between their homes. From his vantage point, it appeared they enjoyed the food and conversation.

Kelly would go north to San Luis Obispo High School where she taught music, and Chimere would head south to Grover Beach.

After a little more than an hour, they would go their separate ways. Chimere would stop at the two local houses then to the office. Her work days typically ended around five, and once a week, she and Felicity would go to nail shop for mani-pedis. At least two or three evenings, the entire family would attend a church function or service. He knew she would be away from the house for at least ten hours, unless she was meeting Kelly or some of the other women from her church for a meeting.

It only took him a month to get down their routines, so he knew he was free to explore. He found out they kept a window slightly opened in the rear of the house. The first time he entered the house, he sat in their casually decorated family room and cried. It was evident this was a well-lived-in family home. The family room had board games neatly placed in a built-in shelf. Next to the board games were several shelves of videos and DVDs of various gospel music artist, popular minister's messages, and movies of almost every genre except horror. The colors throughout the house were warm and inviting. The love of this family enveloped every room and made him not want to leave. On the first visit, he went through the closets and the drawers. From one of her drawers, he selected a pink top from the bottom of a pile. He rubbed the fabric as he sniffed each of the many bottles of perfume. Way in the back he found a bottle of Love's Musky Jasmine perfume, the fragrance she wore every day in college. He saturated the top with the bottle of perfume.

It was evident Medan had been very generous with his gifts. The center of her dresser was consumed by a large jewelry box overflowing with beautiful gold and gemstone pieces. Her mirror was full of love notes and cards. A gold 8 x 10-inch frame of Medan dressed in a tux was placed to the right of the jewelry box. An identical gold frame of her adorned in a wedding gown was on the left. He stood in front of the dresser, pounding his right thigh with all the force he felt reeling inside him. He wanted to throw Medan's picture, but didn't want to disturb them yet. Medan's dresser had several pictures of Chimere with the children: some were current, and some older. Sill pounding his thigh, he went into the walk-in closet. There was not an item of clothing out of place. Everything was color-coordinated for both of them. It seemed Medan had a shirt and tie in every color to match that of Chimere's blouse or dress. When he looked at the shoes, he found a twinge of admiration in Medan's taste. He stood in amazement at the shelves of just basketball shoes. One rack held every NFL Super Bowl championship jersey and several Los Angeles Lakers jerseys. He had suits, slacks, and sports coats in hues of blue, burgundy, brown, green, and black. Another rack was at least twenty or more pairs of denim. His leg began to ache from the steady pounding as he limped out to their bed.

The contents of the night stands made it clear who slept on which side of the bed. Theron ran his hands along the satin bedspread and smoothed out the pillows. He slowly laid himself down on the side of the bed he took to be Chimere's. He pulled one of the pillows from under his head, pushed his face deeply into the center, and took in a deep breath. As he embraced the pillow, tears streamed down his face. He lay in the bed for another ten minutes before he jumped up and continued going through the rooms. He loved the timeline of family photos displayed in the hallway extending into the family room. The hallway was full of pictures of their beginnings in Atlanta. The framed portrait of their wedding day was hung at the entrance. For a moment, he stood in front of the picture of the beautiful couple with a serene ocean background.

He followed the photo timeline through many Christmases, Easters, pregnancies, and other family gatherings. He only spent a minute or two in each the rooms until he reached Tadita's. It seemed as if she had every Barbie in her collection, along with numerous accessories: the beach house, the car, the pool, and several other items for her to play with. The shelves were filled with books and collectable dolls. He smiled as he gazed at the colorful butterflies taking flight around the room. He paused when his eye caught the beautiful portrait of Tadita.

He was in awe at how much this precious little girl looked like Chimere. From her hair to her body shape, she was the spitting image of her mother. All he could think about was how much he wanted to be near all of them. He had to figure out the best plan to remove Medan and take his place in this family he felt should belong to him. This was all he ever wanted, and being with Chimere was all he thought about over the last twenty-six years. Even if it killed him, he was going to find a way to make it happen.

Each room made his chest tighten and his face heat up from all the anger boiling through his veins. The dining room was decorated with a "Happy 25th Anniversary" banner and several bouquets of flowers. In the center of the table were six carefully wrapped gifts. That was all he could stand. He felt his chest getting tighter, and his breathing was strained. He was perspiring profusely and beginning to feel light-headed. He made his way to the front porch and sat on the top step trying to catch his breathe. He glanced at his watch. It was time for the children to be coming home from school, and Medan would be arriving at any moment.

He knew he had to get back to his car before anyone noticed he was lurking around. After settling in the car, he began removing items from under his jacket and his pockets. He had managed to take a small framed photograph of Chimere and the children. He hung the gold locket from the rearview mirror. Carefully, he placed the stuffed orange unicorn and blue Pegasus in the back seat. He knew he better get back to the hotel before Lolita came looking for him.

When he got back to the room he brought his newly acquired items and placed them on the dresser. He placed the photograph on the nightstand on his side of the bed. He quickly removed the pillowcase from his pillow and replaced it with the one he removed from one of Chimere's pillows. He took out some scissors and cut the perfume-saturated shirt into a scarf. As he rubbed the cloth on his cheek, he finally felt close to Chimere again for the first time in over twenty years. The jingling of keys and the fidgeting of the doorknob caught him by surprise. He quickly stuffed his new pink scarf down his shirt. He grabbed the remote to turn on the television and jumped on the bed.

Lolita walked in, carrying bags of groceries and other department store bags. She put some things in the small refrigerator and threw the other bags in the open closet. She grabbed a beer and made her way to the table. She turned to look at Theron who appeared to be engrossed in the television show. As she raised the beer to her mouth, she caught a glimpse of the new picture on the nightstand next to Theron. She stared at the picture until her eyes burned with tears. For the first time in the ten years, she wanted to walk away simply to stop the pain, but her love for Theron and the fear of being without him was paralyzing.

She hoped once he saw how firmly committed and bonded the Freemans were, she and Theron would be able to move on and start a new life together. It had been hard enough telling him about the first two miscarriages. In her mind, she was sure if she would just give him a child of his own, they would have a happy home like, the one he was intent on coveting. This time, she hoped this pregnancy would come to term. Making it through the first trimester was a sign for her this time would be the one. Giving her ammunition to move their relationship forward and for him to stop chasing an unattainable dream.

She prayed his finding out about the plans Medan and Chimere had for their anniversary weekend would somehow give him a jolt back to reality—a reality that would finally make him ready to move on with her. She was determined to make this a special night for them. She had already begun preparing all of his favorite foods. She was excited about giving him the good news about them having a baby and had wrapped the ultrasound photo. Deep down, she was hoping it might just shock Theron and bring him to her completely.

She had found a nice set of matching plates at the little thrift store across from the Jack in the Box. She had stopped at Rite-Aid for half a gallon of pistachio ice cream—his favorite. Her last stop before going back to the small studio was Trader Joe's. She was quickly growing fond of the Five Cities area. The little place they had found near the beach gave her peace and a serenity she had not experienced before. Coming from Atlanta, being this close to the ocean was much better than she had imagined.

She had never really imagined leaving Atlanta, but California was proving to be a great new experience. She especially loved how quaint the cities were and the historical richness of the Mission San Luis Obispo de Tolosa, though she wasn't quite sure what to think of Bubblegum Alley. It was disgusting to think about all the spit and bacteria in all those wads of chewed gum stuck on the walls. The mere fact it has remained there for so long gave her the strong sense of tradition in this small but beautiful college community. The more she explored the area, the more she understood why the Freemans were so entrenched and settled in the area.

She found several old newspaper articles about Chimere, her mother-in-law, and Heart of a Mother homes for unwed pregnant girls. The entire family seemed to be well-known and loved by the entire community. Medan was part of a group of men, who offered their services for free to single mothers in the community. The group was called the Vineyard. They had acquired a large space to use as a garage for repairing and maintaining the vehicles of those in need of repair. The group would hold weekly carwashes, bake sales, and pancake breakfasts to raise funds. Many of the men, who were less mechanically inclined, mentored the young boys. The group found it disheartening how few men of color were willing to become big brothers.

The push to get more men involved was more necessary for this portion of ministry than getting brothers to help with car maintenance and household repairs. They formed volleyball, softball, and football teams for both boys and girls, which was extremely successful. The two divisions were doing well in their classes, and the clubhouse trophy cabinet was bursting with all the awards. The community was always excited at the annual awards dinner and concert. The men loved the opportunity for their choir to give back a little of what God had blessed them with.

Medan had been elected to be the chairman of the group for the last decade. It was under his leadership the mission of the group expanded to the mentorship programs. Medan had always believed the church was lacking and falling short in meeting all the needs in the community. He wanted to be not just a churchgoer but a *Christ-doer*. He chose the Vineyard's slogan from the scripture Psalm 34:10, "The young lions do lack, and suffer hunger: but they that seek the Lord shall not want any good thing." He took Malachi 3:10 a step further than most churches. He felt God didn't mean for all the storehouses to be full just for the keepers of it, but to be distributed to those in need. He disliked it when leadership touted living in the lap of luxury, while the rest of the body was living in lack. He wanted to bring all he had into the storehouse and distribute it to those who had less. He wanted the Vineyard to be the open window, where all who had need of it could come and be fed.

He had even got some of the men at his job to join him. The ones who surprised him with their efforts were the ones not affiliated with any church. These men would donate more money and time than some of the brothers he was in fellowship with. The end result was all Medan needed for single mothers and their children to see a loving God using regular people to help meet their needs. He loved the idea had come to him in a dream, and a conversation with Chimere was the confirmation he needed all those years ago.

It was after their fifth anniversary he knew, without a doubt, what a perfect choice she was for him. She had the heart of a true woman of God, even before she really embraced being a follower of Christ. She had a heart for the young mothers and often spent nights at one of the three Heart of a Mother locations. Medan was proud of the choice he made and grateful to have found such a beautiful wife, inside and out. His feelings for her grew deeper with every passing moment, and he couldn't imagine his life without her.

Their biggest fight was during her pregnancy with Tadita when the Doctor told her to slow down. She wasn't going to slow down, and it wasn't surprising when she went into labor at one of the locations. Felicity was the proudest of her daughter-in-law. She was grateful Chimere came in with an eager heart and zest for the mission and purpose of Heart of a Mother. Chimere had come in and developed more successful programs and funding for them than Felicity had ever imagined. The thing Felicity found most impressive about Chimere was her ability to come into a new situation, grab hold of the mission and vision, and bring it to manifestation in a short time.

The family bond was stronger and more solid than Theron could fathom. As much as he tried to find a weak link, he was unsuccessful. He followed Medan for months, trying to find something he could use to cause a riff in the seemingly unbreakable union. He tried to send women to entice Medan, which were all met with a dignified rejection. Almost all the women reported Medan would speak with them, but the conversation would always end with an invitation to church. Theron would sit outside of the home, watching the many celebrations and family holidays with a burning envy. All his plotting and planning were futile and would send him into a slump for a few days. He knew there had to be a way to come between them and have Chimere all to himself again. He longed for the days back in college when he would see her smiling face every day, when he could get just close enough to smell the sweet scent of the musky Jasmine perfume she wore often.

As difficult as it was to admit, the years had been bountiful for the Freemans. It hurt him deeply when Lolita would try to convince him it was a waste of time. He was troubled by her involvement at the church and the relationship she had developed with the children. Her taking on the role of

Sunday school teacher had been unexpected, but he knew it would give way to the next phase of his plan.

The night of their twenty-fifth anniversary had to be the way in finally. The party was larger than he had thought. He was envious of the support and love they were shown. He sat outside the house, watching the people coming dressed in their finest apparel. He was even a little excited to see the new Harley motorcycle Medan had purchased for Chimere. He was surprised at how much Chimere had changed in the passing years, but he felt certain once he held her in his arms, she would be willing to leave this life behind for the plans he had for them. The celebration lasted well into the early morning hours.

The roar of the motorcycles woke him the next morning. He watched as Medan's mother loaded up the children and Medan packed the saddlebags on the bikes. He overheard Medan speaking to Jim about the route they would be taking to Monterey. When Medan went in the house, Theron decided to get a head start, so he would be in position at a straight portion of the highway. As he waited off the side of the road on Highway 1, all he could hope for was this would be the end of his quest, leaving him the victor and have Chimere as his prize. When he saw them approaching, he started to pull off the shoulder on to the highway. He waited until Medan had passed him before he swerved out into the highway. He heard the screeching of brakes, and in his rearview mirror, the image of the bike flipping and sliding made his heart skip a beat.

He looked ahead of him and saw Medan spin around and race to the spot where Chimere's bike had come to a full stop. He dumped his bike and ran to the side of the road where his wife lay still. He could feel the panic in Medan's voice as he made the call for emergency assistance. Not wanting to be spotted, Theron sped off. He pulled over at a higher location, so he could see what was happening through his high-powered binoculars. As the sirens got closer, the tears rolled down his face. This wasn't how he planned it. Chimere was supposed to stop, and he would grab her. He hadn't intended for her to lose control. He cried as he watched the paramedics work on Chimere. He watched as Medan sat on the side of the road, crying. He was almost ready to abandon the plan when Kelly, Jim, and Medan's parents showed up to help move the bikes off the highway. This was just a minor setback; he would just have to move on to plan B.

Theron had been sitting in the hospital waiting room watching Medan and his children, grateful Medan was so distraught, he hadn't noticed him. Not that he would, because Theron now wore a shaggy beard and dreadlocks, which completely transformed from the clean-shaven look of their college days. He kept his shades on to cover his bloodshot eyes and the scar over his left brow. As he watched the two beautiful daughters clinging and embracing him, his anger boiled. *Those should have been my children!* The affection being poured on Medan should have been his. Medan stole his life. Chimere belonged to him. He was going to have her no matter what it took.

In the meantime, he was captivated with the youngest girl. He heard them call her Tadi. She was a miniature Chimere, golden brown with wild light brown curly hair with thick black lashes surrounded by large ebony eyes. He loved watching her when the restlessness would overtake her and she would gracefully dance around the small waiting room. He was amazed at how coordinated and graceful little Tadi was. In the small area near her dad, she never lost her balance when she was twirling nor stumbled when she did her leaps.

Medan would let her dance when the waiting room was empty. When his sisters came, one of them would read one of Tadi's favorite books to settle her down. He knew he would have to send the children back to school soon, but right now, he needed his babies around him.

Theron was intrigued by how obedient and committed the children were when Medan would make them circle up to pray. As Medan would often get choked up, Obadiah would complete the prayer without any lapse, all the while holding his sister Maja as she wept on his shoulder. The unity of this family hurt Theron's stomach. He should have been the man these children were supporting. He did feel a little guilty the family was here. This wasn't how he thought things would turn out. The accident was just supposed to be a diversion, so he could grab Chimere and take her away.

He never meant for her to be hurt. All he wanted was her. He didn't know how much longer he would be able to wait.

Watching all the various visitors come and form prayer circles was beginning to irritate Theron. He would sit close enough to Medan and the children, so he could hear the doctor's prognosis. His heart would stop every time the doctor would tell the family the only thing keeping her alive were the machines and low brain activity. He had to admire Medan's faith because each time, he would reply with, "No, doctor, I don't accept that! I know my wife is just sleeping and talking to God. You wait, you'll see!"

Over the last few months as Theron observed this family, he found himself being more intrigued by the faith Medan and Chimere had found. He would sit in the very back of the church on most Tuesdays and Sundays. The Pastor or teacher would be delivering words and messages that were completely foreign to him, yet it seemed to spark something in the congregation and the Freeman family. He was coming to enjoy the Sundays when the children were in charge of the services. Listening to Maja sing took his breath away, and it had him in tears a few times. She had the voice of an angel. Although she had some of her mother's features, she looked more like Medan. As difficult as it was to admit, he was gaining real respect for Medan. He was like a watchman, sitting in the pulpit with the other elders. He would watch over the church members, and it was apparent Medan was well-respected. He demonstrated a knowledge of the word and from what Theron could see, he was living what he spoke about.

After every service, he would go back to the studio he was sharing with Lolita so she could give him more details on Chimere. It excited him when he'd catch a glimpse of Tadita, hugging or sitting on Lolita's lap. It made him feel much closer to Chimere, even if it was by proxy. All Theron could think about was how he would make this family his. He would sit for hours daydreaming of how wonderful and different his life will be once he'd have Chimere by his side. In all the years he had been searching for Chimere, finding her again was all he had hoped for, only to be disappointed at seeing her very content with the life she had developed with Medan.

After two weeks of waiting for Chimere to come out of her coma, Theron decided he had to change direction, and the next best thing to having Chimere was her baby girl. He knew he needed a little more time. He made all the plans for him to leave and set things up. He gave Lolita specific instructions and made his way out of California. The plan was simple; all Lolita had to do was get Tadita to leave with her after Sunday evening service. If what she had told him about how much Tadita liked her, this would be the easy part. Getting her to cooperate after leaving the church was going to be another task. He had thought it all out. As long as Lolita followed his plan, they would soon be a family.

FINDERS KEEPERS

Lolita was a little hesitant about drugging Tadita, but she knew it would be the only way to travel with her to Los Angeles to catch their flight. What she had not anticipated was Tadita talking in her sleep. At first, she thought it was her way of praying, but the conversations were more than that. It was as if she were being asked questions by someone. When Tadita woke up screaming in the motel room, all Lolita could think of was to drug her again. She knew she only had enough sedatives to last until they reached Houston, and she was worried about the after effects.

The only way to get through the security gates with Tadita was to carry her when she's asleep. She was worried the stress of carrying the little girl would be more than she could handle, and losing her baby just would not work for her. The baby was the only thing she had to use to hold on to the Theron. When Lolita and Tadita landed at a small airport in Hobbs, New Mexico, she knew it was a horrible mistake. How had she allowed Theron to convince her this was a good idea? Tadita had cried the entire hour and a half from Houston. She held her and tried to reassure her she would be home soon. It broke her heart when she lied to Tadita about her mother being dead. What astounded her was Tadita's resolve that her mother wasn't dead and she was having conversations with her.

After they stepped into the warm air of Hobbs, Tadita looked at her and said boldly, "My mommy will find me, and you will be sorry you said she was dead! My mommy loves me and would never leave me like you said. I told her you were nice to me, but I want to go home with my daddy. My mommy will find me!"

When they entered the area to get their luggage, Theron was there waiting for them. This was the first time Lolita had seen Theron without the dreadlocks and the bushy beard. For the first time in years, she saw just how handsome he was. As she watched him grab the suitcases, she remembered why she had been so easily convinced to help this man. His strong jaw, straight wide nose, thick lips, and straight white teeth made it all that much easier to look at him now. She had seen the pictures of him before he'd gone to jail, and over the years, she had watched him turn into a gruff, stubborn man. She knew his obsession with Chimere wasn't good, but she had already fallen in love with him. She thought once he was outside and in her arms, she would be able to convince him Chimere would never be what she could be for him.

When he embraced Tadita and began to weep in her hair, Lolita grabbed the smaller bags and began to walk toward the parking lot. Her heart was aching, and her mind was racing. *What had she gotten herself into? Why was this man so crazy in love with Chimere? Why had she let him talk her into taking this baby away from her family? Was it too late to walk away?* She pushed the thoughts from her mind and placed the bags at the rear of the car, while she waited for Theron and Tadita to get there.

Her cheeks burned with tears of anger and disappointment. She had given up a chance at a normal life to chase after a man who was obsessed with another woman. She had now jeopardized her freedom for the love of a man who was so single-minded, she wasn't even sure how he felt about her. Sure, he had told her once he'd be lost without her, but in all the years she had been visiting and writing him, he never expressed anything other than immense gratitude. She knew in her heart it was wrong, but Theron meant more to her than anything. She wanted him to know just how committed she was to him. Nothing mattered more than to be able to lay with him and share a life with him, even if it was a life on the run.

Theron had found a cute little two-bedroom duplex for them on the southeast side of town. He had found a job with one of the big oil companies. The hours and schedule he had would keep him away from home for three to four days, but the pay enabled him to stop hacking accounts. Now with Tadita finally his, the risk was too great to keep up skimming accounts. He had used the remaining ill-gotten funds to secure the duplex, furnish it, and purchase a second vehicle for Lolita to get around the small city.

He was off for the next two days, so he decided to take Lolita on a tour to become familiar with their new home. They went off after lunch taking Lovington Highway to as far as the College of the Southwest. They drove through the casino parking lot then headed to the east side of town, where all the less desirables were located. They saw several hookers hanging out at the Hobbs Inn. They stopped by at Wal-Mart to grab some of the household items. Theron still felt a little overwhelmed when shopping. It was one thing to be able to geek out on a computer, but being in stores and seeing it firsthand was like stepping into a time warp. There were so many wondrous innovative gadgets there; too many choices made his head swim. He hoped his choice for furnishings would be acceptable for Lolita and Tadita. He had purchased every Barbie doll and all the accessories he could fit in the back of the truck. He made sure her desk had a laptop and a printer. He was hoping filling her room with toys and gadgets would allow him a little space in her heart.

She was to Theron more like her mother than she could even imagine. The only difference now was he had money and would be able to buy his way into her heart. She was young and still very easily charmed, so he was on his way to his wish being fulfilled. He had searched and searched for Chimere, and even though he had to settle for Tadita, he knew that with enough time and loads of gifts, she would love him. She would not cast him aside for another man. After some time, she would bond with him as a father, and she would be his always.

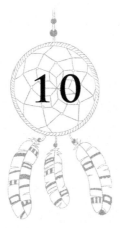

BEYOND BORDERS

After three months, Tadita seemed be adjusting to being with them. She was warming up once again to Lolita, but she pulled away from Theron all the time.

One morning, Lolita hadn't been feeling well so Theron decided to let her remain in bed. Theron wasn't ready for what was in store this morning when he was in charge of taking Tadi to school. He had made sure to fix all of her favorites for breakfast and put a little extra snack in her lunch. Hoping this would be the break the wall Tadi had, he went to wake her. He walked into her room to find Tadi sitting on her bed and fully dressed with her backpack on.

"Good morning, Tadi. I hope you slept well. Well, this is a nice surprise. Glad you are all ready to go. Come on, I fixed your favorite, French toast with strawberry syrup."

"Thank you, Mr. Ron, but I'm not really hungry. My name is Tadita. Only my family calls me Tadi. When are you going to take me home? My mommy is missing me so much, and she wants to wake up. She is very angry with you, you know? She told me to tell you this is not going to work. You are a very bad man! I don't like you, and I don't like it here. I want to go home, so my mommy can wake up!"

He stood at the door and looked at this little girl with her hands on her hips, speaking to him as if she were an adult. He was amazed at the intelligence the seven-year-old showed and how calmly she expressed herself to him. He was proud of her yet angry she took that tone with him.

"Well, young lady, you really shouldn't tell lies. When exactly did you speak to your mother?"

"I speak to my mother every night. She comes to me every night and sings to me. I dance for her and make her smile, because she is missing me so much. My brother and sister are sad too. You better hope my daddy doesn't get a hold of you, and mommy hopes he doesn't because he will kill you for this."

"That's a very nice story, Tadita, and you know that's not possible. Your mother is in a very deep sleep, and she doesn't know where you are. I told you your father told me I could take you, because he wasn't able to care for you while your mother is in the hospital."

"That's not true! My daddy would never let someone have me. My daddy loves me, and Nanna would have taken care of me, I'm sure of it. My mommy *does* know where I am. I told her to look for the water tower, and she will find me."

"That's enough, Tadita! Let's get you fed and off to school. Lolita will pick you up after school and take you shopping. Would that make you feel better?"

"I don't want to go shopping, I want to go home. I've been a good girl. I kept my promise, and I haven't told anyone the truth at school or anywhere else. Please, Mr. Ron, take me home! I'll be your best friend if you take me home. I promise to tell my daddy how good you treated me so he won't hurt you."

"Come on, go eat your breakfast. We can talk about this more later."

Frustrated and angry, Theron went into the kitchen and banged the pan on the counter. He served Tadita her French toast and chocolate milk. He went into the room to check on Lolita, while Tadita ate her meal.

"Lolita, does Tadita tell you stories about having conversations with her mother?"

"Yes, she has. But I just tell her it's not possible and telling stories is a bad thing, even though she insists Chimere and some boy named 'Ready Eddie' talk to her every night. She is a very smart little girl. She even told me we are having a boy and will name him Darnell. That little girl frightens me sometimes, Ronnie. She seems to know things, and it scares me. She talks about her mother like she is really talking to her. Babe, please…can't we just take her back then come back here and raise our baby?"

"Chi—Lolita, stop being foolish. She is only seven. What could she possibly know? It's obvious she has a very good imagination. We both know Chimere is still on life support and in a deep coma. Anyway, how could they possibly talk? It's not like we are in a notable city. Hobbs is way off anyone's trail. There is no way. So stop feeding into her make-believe. I know this stress is not good for the baby. I'll be back in a little bit, let me get her off to school."

"Ronnie, I'm really worried. What if she tells one of her classmates? What if—"

"Lolo, stop it, please! Get some rest, and I'll come fix you a good hearty breakfast when I get back."

"I'll try, but you need to know I'm really worried. I love you, Ronnie."

"Yeah, okay. Get some rest. Be back in a few."

He leaned down, kissed her on the forehead, and patted her on the head. He left the room so quickly Lolita didn't get to ask him to stop by Albertson's to grab a few things.

As much as she wanted to walk away from this whole situation, she felt trapped. If she walked away now, she would be losing everything she had invested the last twenty years of her life into. If she tried to leave now, she was risking the life of their child and, very possibly, her own as well. She had loved Theron from the moment they met. How could she leave him? He was all she'd loved and known for so long. In her mind, even the thought of being arrested or if they were caught wasn't enough to leave him. She hadn't left him when he was in jail and wouldn't do so now. Lolita didn't mind being confined in this little town. For her, the highlight of most days was seeing some strange sight at Wal-Mart. After the few talk shows she enjoyed, daytime television wasn't for her.

Tadita was a great help to her. After school, she would make sure the house was tidy. Tadita would bring her homework to wherever Lolita was resting to share every lesson with her. It was a comfort for Lolita, because her heart ached for this little girl. She could see behind her sweet smile she was hurting. Even her little hugs were weak and listless.

"Tadita, you know you don't have to clean the house. You know I have someone coming in three times a week. You don't have to sit here and do your homework every day. That's why I found you that nice little desk."

"My momma told me chores are important, and she tells me which ones to do every day. Thank you for the desk, but I'm teaching Baby Darnell. He likes it. It's okay if you don't want to listen, you will understand more very soon. I pray for you all every night. God is taking care of it all."

"Tadita, you really are a sweet little girl. I'm sorry you miss your family, but Theron is my family and I can't lose him. You understand, right? Once the baby is born, I promise things will change. Once he has a baby of his own, he'll lose—um…anyway, are you making any friends yet?"

"I have friends at home, but I do talk to the kids sometimes. Mostly to the Mexican ones though. They help me with my Spanish, and I help them with English. Maja used to help me with my Spanish. I miss her doing my hair too." Tadita slumped down into the chair as tears rolled down her cheeks. "My homework is finished. Can we watch some Disney Channel now?"

Lolita reached for her, but she slouched deeper into the chair. She got the remote and changed the channel to Disney. They sat there, silently watching for some time before Lolita dozed off. Tadita watched her favorite shows for a while until Lolita would wake up and take control.

This routine was the same for them every day. Tadita didn't mind it, because Theron was gone most of the time. It was rare she would sit still when he would try to hug and play with her hair. His touch made her flesh crawl. She looked forward to making him angry, because she would pull away from him. He would send her to her room sometimes when she refused to sit next to him. She liked it best when he worked. Lolita was nice enough, and she liked talking to her about the new baby.

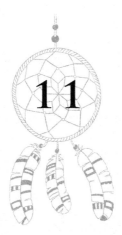

PROMISE KEEPER

The ringing of the phone woke Medan up from a deep sleep. Groggily, he answered the phone. He just sat listening to the voice on the other end. He tossed the phone and immediately dropped to his knees. Not waking the children wasn't a concern for him at that moment. He could hear the nurse on the other end of the line calling his name, but he owed God too much for what the nurse had called a miracle.

Chimere had opened her eyes and was asking for him. The nurse explained she was a little disoriented but very much awake and alert.

"Mr. Freeman, are you still there?"

"Yes, yes, I'm still here. Sorry, I had to take a minute to give praise and honor to God. This is, in fact, a pure demonstration of his power and the power of faithful prayer."

"Yes, sir, this is indeed a miracle. The doctor wants to run some test, but from what he saw this morning, all her muscles and mental state are normal. The only concern is some of the things she is saying. She told us to call the police. She said she knows where her baby is and something about a tan water tower."

"Tan water tower? That's okay. I'll be there as soon as I can. Thank you, Nurse Bryant. Thank you so much!"

He hung up the phone and ran down the hallway, shouting for the children to get up. They both came into the hallway rubbing the sleep from their eyes. Obadiah went and put his arm around his sister's shoulders, waiting for what he thought was news about Tadita. Maja looked at her brother, and they both looked at their father.

"Papa, what is it? Did they find Tadi? When is she coming home? Do they know who took her?" Maja asked anxiously.

Medan struggled to compose himself. He was so ecstatic to know the love of his life was finally awake, he'd almost forgotten about his baby girl being gone. He grabbed his children and hugged them tightly.

"Oh, baby, I'm sorry. No, they haven't found our Tadi yet. Mommy is awake and asking for us. I need you both to hurry up and get dressed. I want to get to the hospital right away. I'm going to call Nanna and Pop-Pop, so they can meet us. Mommy is awake! Thank you, Jesus. Mommy is awake and waiting for her family."

Obadiah feel to his knees and began to praise God. Maja and Medan joined him just as he was beginning to pray.

"Father God, I come before you with a humble heart and joy unspeakable. You have, once again, shown our family your favor, and we are grateful for your healing virtue touching our mother. Thank you for protecting her mind, body, and soul, while she rested in your arms. Thank you, Lord, for your favor and great love. We love you, Lord, not for just this miracle, but for giving us this glorious testimony of your power and mercy. We are grateful for your unconditional love. We thank you for shining down on our family. We ask you to give our mother the strength to hear about her baby. We know you are watching over and protecting Tadita. We know if you are able to fulfill this promise, we can stand strong in faith our little Tadi will be home soon. Thank you for this glorious day. We give you all the praise, all the honor, and all the glory. In Jesus's name. Amen"

They stood and held hands. Maja seemed to be in a trance, and then suddenly, she began to sing "He's Keeping Me". She was weeping and jumping with joy as she sang, allowing the spirit to take control. Her voice seemed to echo throughout the house as if she were singing with an amplifier. After she sang the last verse, she fell into her father's open arms. Medan held his little girl as she wept, whispering repeatedly thanks to God.

"Alright, I know this is great news, but let's get to steppin! Momma is waiting for us. It has been a long nine months, and I need to hear her voice. So let's get it together, and go see Momma."

"Okay, Papa." The children replied in unison as they headed back to their rooms to get dressed.

Medan stood in the hallway and watched his children rush off to their rooms. He lifted his arms and gave God one more thanks. He went into his room, sat on the end of their bed, and wept. After a few minutes, he picked up his cell phone and called his mother.

"Mommy, did I wake you?"

"Hey, baby boy! Now you know you didn't wake me. I was enjoying my quiet time with God. What's wrong, son?"

He was silent for a moment as the tears began to flow again. "Mommy, she's awake…Oh, thank you, Jesus! Chimere is awake. The nurse said she was a little disoriented, but she is awake. The kids and I are heading out to the hospital now. Can you and Dad meet us there?"

Felicity shouted and dropped the phone. "Thank you, God! Thank you, Lord!" She picked up the phone with tears in her eyes. "Of course we will meet you there. I'll call her parents. You just get to her, son."

"All right, Mommy. I love you. See you all there. Thank you, Mommy!"

Medan quickly grabbed a jacket and his keys. Much to his surprise, Maja and Obadiah were already in the car waiting for him. He smiled when looked out the front door to see them hanging out the car windows, waving for him to come. He heard Obadiah shout for him to hurry. He laughed as he made his way to the car.

They arrived at the hospital, and the atmosphere was bubbling with the excitement of the miracle. When he and the children arrived at Chimere's room, his parents, along with Jim and Kelly, were already there crying and laughing. Chimere seemed to glow when he walked in. She was sitting up with her arms outstretched to hold her children. Looking at her was proof that God was smiling on his wife. She looked as beautiful as she did the day he saw her all those years ago.

The phone in the room rang seemingly every time Chimere would hang up from one call. The nurses kept coming in with bouquets of flowers and just looking in awe, while Chimere reassured them she was doing well. Medan overheard a couple of the nurses discussing how miraculous this was and how amazed they were by his family's faith. It made Medan smile and silently give thanks and praise for this day. After about an hour, everyone decided to go to Scrambles for breakfast.

Medan told them he would meet them later at the house. He wanted to spend as much time with the love of his life as he could. He was glad no one brought up Tadita, but he knew it was something Chimere needed to discuss. After all the hugs and kisses, he closed the door and climbed into bed with his wife.

Chimere looked at her husband and held him as he wept on her bosom. She rubbed his head and whispered, "It's okay, my love. I'm here, and I'm fine. Thank you for not giving up on me."

He lifted his head and kissed her gently on the lips. "How could I ever give up on you Chi-Chi? Giving up on you would be like giving up on myself. We are one, and I wouldn't even know how to move forward without you. You and the children are all I ever wanted. Baby, I had no choice but to trust that God would keep his promise. It was a fight to believe *God is not a man that he should lie* when I would come here and see you just lying in this bed. It was a struggle to have faith until God heard my continuous pleas for your return. No matter how dreadful the situation was, all I could hear was God saying to me to be of good courage. 'This illness is not unto death.' Chimere, I love you, baby. Happy belated Anniversary! Well, one good thing about this is now we can begin again."

"Medan, you are the most wonderful husband. I know this was difficult for all of you, but I knew as I lay here God had a purpose for all of this. I knew you were here every day. I heard your prayers and pleas to God, but it just wasn't time for me to speak. I know they haven't found the person that caused me to dump my bike. I also know who took Tadita. What I am about to tell you is going to blow your mind, but I need you to hear me out before you say anything."

Medan took both of Chimere's hands and laid his head on her shoulder. "Okay, sweetie. I'm listening with a clear head and heart. I want to know who took our baby more than you can imagine, so tell me everything!"

Chimere moved her shoulder to get his head off. "Honey, I need you to look at me when I tell you this. Let's see…Let me take you back to the night at the party before graduation. You called him 'that Alpha dude' and some other expletive. Anyway, his name is Theron Dunkle. What I didn't know then was he had this crush on me that was deeper than I realized. I suppose you could say he is completely obsessed with me. After the beating, I began having these dreams. Remember the dream you had that Christmas? Well, the boy who came to you had been coming to me for months, along with several other young men. All of whom, I found out later, were murdered during the 1984 Atlanta Child Murders."

She stopped for moment and looked into her husband's face. Medan had a puzzled look on his face as she continued. "I know this sounds absolutely insane, honey, but these boys told me so many details about what had happened to them, what it felt like as they had their last breath, and how much better they were. They all wanted me to deliver a message to their families. They would disturb my sleep to persuade me to tell their loved ones they were fine and they loved them.

It frightened me and amazed me, all at the same time. I even went to a physic hoping for help, and thankfully, the dream visits did stop. However, you know you've always asked me how I knew certain things? Well, the truth is, after the visits from the boys stopped, I began to have dreams in which angels would give me messages. I need you to know one very important thing—our baby is fine. She is smarter than we know. God blessed me while I was sleeping. He allowed me to watch over and communicate with Tadi every day. She would tell me about her days at school and how much she was missing all of you. She has been very brave. You should be proud of her. She reminds me of you in so many ways.

"Okay, I've strayed a little from the point. She is in a small town in New Mexico. Theron—and this woman he's with—took her because she was the closest thing to being with me as he could get. It was his car that ran me off the road. It wasn't his plan for me to be hurt. He had hoped I would have stopped, and then he was going to grab me. Taking Tadi was the alternative and a last resort. Tadi has been giving me as much information as possible about the location. Look in that drawer and grab my notebook. I need you to call the agent in charge who has the resources at his disposal to determine the exact city. From the list Tadi gave me, there are streets she was able to write down as the woman took her to and from school, shopping malls, and parks where she played. I am so proud of this little girl of ours. From the very first time I was transported to her, she felt me. She knew I was there and began speaking to me just like we would do before our early morning prayers. She was not afraid at all. She told me she'd prayed for God to let her talk to me. Her faith in our love for her and in God astounded me. She is more beautiful with every passing day. She dances for me, and she actually sings quite well. The reason—I think—that I couldn't wake up before was because our daughter needed me. It seems unrealistic even to me, and I've been experiencing it. The only thing I know is the angels and our daughter kept me busy these last several months."

Medan looked at his wife and then exploded with laughter. He shook his head and took Chimere's face in his hands. He gently kissed her lips again and smiled at the baffled look on her face. "Chimere, here we thought your waking up was a miracle, but you *are* a miracle! You have been speaking to angels all these years and managed to keep that a secret. You have not kept a secret from me since you finally told me about Theron. I love you, woman! I just have one question, why didn't you come to me in my dreams? I was praying for the same thing Tadi was. All I wanted was to hear your voice again."

He stood and started gathering some of the flowers. He looked around the room as tears began to warm his cheeks. With his hands full, he stood over her and kissed her on the forehead. "Baby, I have the list and will call Agent

Wymond. No, better yet, I'll call him as soon as I get in the office. You get some rest, and I'll be back later this evening."

He kissed her again and left the room. He was smiling from ear to ear as he said good-bye to the nurses as he passed them. He had a spring in his step he hadn't felt for months. He was so full at this moment, it was hard for him to not just stop and shout out a hallelujah. God was true to His word. Not once during Chimere's *sleep* did he feel alone. Although it was difficult not having her next to him every night and his heart hurt, he always felt the presence of God. He had no doubt in everything Chimere had told him. He was just happy thinking about the end of this trial. He rejoiced all the way to work for the gift and return of his true love.

When he got into the office, the first thing he did was go on the internet and began looking up some of the items on the list Chimere had made. The first thing he found was there were over two hundred cities with water towers in New Mexico. He knew this task was bigger than he could undertake and decided to call Agent Wymond. Although he wanted to be the one to bring his baby home, this was more than he was able to do alone.

"Wymond."

"Good morning, Agent Wymond! Medan Freeman here. My wife just woke from her coma and said some pretty spectacular stuff. She has a list of things I think you need to look at. If I told you everything, you would think I was completely delusional or that my wife was."

"Hello Medan, I was just going to give you a call. I'm sorry I haven't been in touch, but we have no new leads. Glad to hear your wife is awake. I would love to speak with her. I could meet you at the hospital after you get off work. In the meantime, send me the stuff she gave you, and I'll see if they are of any help. Off the record, Medan, I had a dream just last night, and the angel told me this case was going to be over and *our* prayers are answered. I have faith the information Chimere gave you will be exactly the missing link we need to bring your baby girl home."

"Agent Wymond, can I be really honest with you? When you were assigned our case nine months ago, I had an immediate sense of relief. I knew deep in my soul you would be the one to never give up. I thank you for all you have done. I will meet you in the hospital cafeteria around four. I just emailed you the list. See you later."

"I look forward to seeing you both, Medan. Bye for now."

Medan called his staff into his office. He gave them the news and told them he was going to work from home for a short time. They all rejoiced, and his assistant spoke up for the entire staff.

"Medan, why are you here? You need to go be with your family. We got this, now get out of here." The laughed and hugged each other.

Medan went in his office to grab some work material and headed out, knowing each step was ordered by his heavenly father. He felt like he was twenty-six again. He had the flutter in his stomach knowing he was going to hold Chimere and his children. It wasn't that he expected there to be a problem with his staff, he was just relieved at all the answered prayers. He couldn't seem to get the smile off his face. This was surely the day of rejoicing for his entire family. When he cranked the engine, the sound of Fred Hammond's soulful voice singing "No Weapon" floated in the air. Medan sat there and sang along with the Fred at the top if his lungs. Tears of joy were streaming down his cheeks as he sang the first verse. "God will do what he said he would do. He's not a man that he should lie, He will come through."

When he got to the house, he noticed Jim's truck and his parent's Lexus were parked there. He pulled into the driveway and jumped out of the car. He stepped inside the door and fell to his knees. He couldn't believe what he was seeing, until he felt her tiny hands on his face. The tears blurred his sight, but the joy he was feeling was immeasurable. All he could do was to hug her as tightly as he could without crushing her.

"Papa, you can let go now. I'm not going anywhere."

"Okay, baby, but Papa is just so happy to see you. I missed you so much, sweetheart."

"I know, Papa. Can we go see Momma now?"

"Of course we will go see Momma, but first, tell Papa how you got here."

Jim came over and knelt with them. "She showed up at our door after we got back from Scrambles. She was at the door with a suitcase and a smile that will stay in my mind forever." Jim began to weep when he felt Kelly's arm around his shoulders. "When I opened the door, she just jumped into my arms screaming, 'Uncle Jumbo!' Agent Wymond is on his way. He suggested we wait to question Tadita with all of us together. Mom and Dad Freeman, join us please. Let's pray."

There was a knock on the door. Medan yelled out for whoever it was to come in. Agent Wymond entered with a smile on his face. He greeted every one and knelt down next to Dad Freeman. Jim began to pray as murmurs of thanks rang out in the living room. They spoke in unison at the conclusion of the prayer with a resounding *Amen*!

Medan sat Tadita on the couch and introduced her to Agent Wymond. The agent smiled as she greeted him very politely. She raised her tiny hands and rubbed the side of his face. Agent Wymond got a little choked up at the sincerity he saw in her pretty little face. He was amazed at the peace and calm of a little girl who had been snatched from her family. More than that, he was anxious to find out how she got home.

Still smiling, Tadita began to speak. "Papa, the man, who took me, put me on a plane last night. He told me to tell you he was sorry for putting our family through so much pain and *aglewish*."

They all giggled. Medan nodded his head and told her the correct word.

"Anguish. I heard him and Lolita fighting that evening. Lolita had a dream that their baby would die if they didn't take me back home that minute. Anyway, Mr. Ron told me to pack my bag, and we drove to Lubbuck and took a flight to LA. We drove here in a rented car, he dropped me off at Uncle Jumbo's, and left."

"Where did he go, Tadita? Can you tell us how he looks now and what kind of car you all drove to get here?" Agent Wymond probed.

If he could get a good description of Thereon and car, they may just apprehend him before he reached Los Angeles and the airport. After he met the Freemans, he was glad he had been the agent in charge of this case. It was more than just another stolen child, he knew it was a case God meant for him to handle. It was the case to open his eyes more to the real wonders God still preformed in this age. He took down all the details Tadita was able to give him. He asked her for a hug and promised he would make sure Theron and Lolita would go to jail for taking her away from her family.

Tadita placed her hand on his cheek again and smiled. "Mr. Wymond, God said vengeance is his. I'm home now, and he is already dealing with Mr. Ron and Lolita. Putting them behind bars and depriving their child of both parents is not the answer. If it will make you feel better to bring them in, then you do your job. I promised Lolita no one would take her baby away. They didn't hurt me, and I don't want to hurt them. I forgive them for taking me, and they were really, really nice to me."

Agent Wymond wanted to give this little girl her wish, but he was obligated to perform his duty first. He put out the bulletin to California Highway Patrol of the car being driven by Theron. He looked at Tadita and told her he would do what he could to keep Lolita out of it, unless Theron mentioned her involvement to other law enforcement agents.

Tadita went to him, smiled, then gave him a hug. They all thanked him for all his kindness and help. After the agent had left, they all jumped in their cars and headed off to the hospital. Medan had to catch himself when he realized he was driving over a hundred on the freeway. The kids were enjoying him weaving in and out of traffic. They wanted to see their mother as much as he did, but they were more excited about their mother seeing their little sister.

They arrived at the hospital before everyone else and raced to Chimere's room.

Medan opened the door to find Chimere dressed and packed up. He looked at the smile on her face and understood it to mean that she already knew.

"Where is my baby girl, Papa? I know she's here."

"Momma, I'm right here, just like I told you I would be."

Puzzled, Maja and Obadiah looked at each other, then at their mother and baby sister. The two slowly walked toward each other. Tadita leaped into her mother's arms. Chimere caught her and began to dance around the room with her daughter snuggly in her arms. Tears streamed down her cheeks with each whirl around the room. Medan joined them, embracing both his daughter and his wife. They danced for a few moments when the nurse came in.

She smiled and joined the family in the applause. She hugged Chimere and left after the release papers were signed.

They gathered up the remaining flowers, balloons, and stuffed toys. They were all full of joy and praise as they departed, waving farewell to all the wonderful nurses and aides. Medan rolled the wheelchair to the elevator then leaned over and kissed Chimere on the top of her head. When they reached the entrance, the cluster of reporters was milling around waiting for them.

Medan stopped and looked at his family. For sure, this was a story to be told, but this wasn't the way he'd had in mind to share this wonderful testimony. He looked at his wife and knew she wasn't ready to face the flashing lights and barrage of questions. His parents and Jim and Kelly waited a few minutes for them to reach the side entrance before they distracted the aggressive reporters. He turned the wheelchair toward the side entrance and briskly walked his family out.

Mr. Freeman decided to take the lead with the reporters. "Today, our daughter-in-law has fully recovered by the mercies of God. She is fully healed, and when she has had a chance to be with her family, I'm sure she will give you all a little time. Our family is in awe of how truly blessed we are and at the favor of a living God. Not only did we get to begin our day with the news of Chimere waking, but our beautiful Grandbaby was returned to us today. We ask you give us time to reunite before we give you the whole story. We thank you all for your prayers, and we will give the story in its entirety."

Medan honked the horn as they drove off. They were relieved when they arrived at their home, no reporters had made it there. Once they closed all the curtains and blinds to keep peeping eyes out, they gathered in the family room. The evening was filled with everyone trying to catch up. Chimere reassured her family she knew everything, because she had been aware of every conversation they had when visiting her.

The phone rang several times before Medan decided to answer. He was grateful the voice on the other end was their Pastor. They spoke for a few moments before Medan hung up. "Well, Pastor just asked me to deliver the message next Sunday. I don't think he asked the right one of us to do this. I'm not a preacher. I wouldn't even know what to say."

"My love, you shouldn't wonder what to say until you've had some quiet time with God to ask him. I'll be right in the front pew to encourage you."

"Yes, Papa, we will all be in the front cheering you on. You got this, Papa!" Obadiah chimed in.

"Well, all right then. If my family believes I can do this, then I know I can. He didn't even give me a theme or anything, so I guess you're right, honey. I better check in with God."

"Then let's pray right now Papa. Let's join hands." Obadiah stood in the middle of the family room floor with, his arms extended waiting for the family to join him. "Come on, momma, you too. You need to lead us in this prayer for Papa."

They could hear the commotion in front but didn't want to stop what was needed to be done. The shouting grew louder as Jim, Kelly, and Medan's parents struggled to get past the now growing crowd of reporters camped on the front lawn. They laughed and sighed after they managed to finally get the door closed. Once everyone was in the circle, Chimere looked around and began to weep. She tried to find her voice, but her joy was full and the tears wouldn't stop.

Medan squeezed her hand and kissed her cheek. "Chimere and I are one, so everyone, please bow your heads and clear your minds... Lord, we come to you in complete gratitude for this day. We thank you, Lord, for showing your miraculous ways and power over all the things, which—by our sight—we thought impossible. Thank you for bringing us all together on this day to be a witness of your power and grace. Lord, we ask that you open our ears for us to hear more clearly and open our eyes so we may see you clearly. We surrender to your will to be a vessel and share what you showed us without hesitation. We are grateful for your healing love. We thank you for your strength in our times of weakness. Thank you for keeping us holding on to the promise that no weapon formed will bring any harm against us. We ask you continue to bring the increase of your knowledge, as we gladly move forward in ministering to others. We thank you for total healing in every area of our lives, as we give you all the honor and all the praise. We thank and praise you with a full heart and a humble spirit. We pray these things in your precious son, Jesus's name."

In unison, the family shouted, "Amen!"

The phone rang again just as they were finished with prayer. This time, Chimere answered. "Hello, Agent Wymond! We didn't expect to hear from you so soon. Yes... oh, that is great news... Yes, Tadita is right here with me. I will be sure to tell her. Thank you so much for all your help. God bless you!" Chimere hung up the phone and pulled Tadita to her. "Agent Wymond wants you to know Theron can't hurt you or come near you anymore. He says he will be flying to New Mexico tomorrow to speak with Lolita and do whatever he can to keep her from being charged as an accomplice. Theron is taking full responsibility for taking you and moving you across state lines. He said he did it all alone. It's over, and we don't have to worry about him being in our lives anymore. He will be going to federal prison for a very long time."

She hugged her baby and wept as she looked around the room at all the love standing before her: the lifelong friends, Jim and Kelly, and her wonderful in-laws. All she could think of was how grateful she was and how much time had gone by while she was speaking with angels and traveling with them. They watched over each of her family members, while they thought she was asleep. Chimere now had a peace about her gift; she was no longer running from it. She now saw with understanding of a God she still had not seen with the natural eye.

She felt she was now an evidence of the existence and love of something greater than what man could ever conceive. She was to be a testament of God not changing in his modes of operation, no matter how some men tried to persuade this age of the necessity of a new and different way to get people's attention. A living witness of Hebrews

13:8 "Jesus Christ the same **yesterday**, and to day, and for ever." A heart full of knowing God did it for Joseph, He did it for Job, and He did it for her in a way she never would have imagined possible. Super God was over the natural. She was no longer asleep. She had fresh new oil and was now ready to share it with others of little faith.

From this moment on, she knew the lives of the Freemans would never be the same. The family began to bustle in the kitchen to prepare a celebration dinner.

Chimere picked up the phone. "Hi, Daddy! God told me to tell you, 'Well done, my good and faithful servant'. It was because of you and Mommy praying I am awake. Thank you, Daddy." Her father was silent. She knew he was weeping. A few moments later, she heard her mother's voice, and she got choked up. They spoke for a moment before her parents let her know they were on their way.

Chimere stood in the entry of the kitchen, watching the loves in her life move in a boundless joy once again. She was amazed at how God had changed her life and was anxious to see what He could possible do to top this. Whatever it was, she was saying yes. Yes, to her purpose and yes to His love.

Today, she was a living witness to Joel 2:28: "And it shall come to pass afterward, that I will pour out my spirit upon all flesh; and your sons and your daughters shall prophesy, your old men shall dream dreams, your young men shall see visions."

CPSIA information can be obtained
at www.ICGtesting.com
Printed in the USA
LVOW04s0055221016
509645LV00011B/130/P